SECRET IN ST. SOMETHING

Aladdin Paperbacks by
BARBARA BROOKS WALLACE

The Barrel in the Basement
Cousins in the Castle
Ghosts in the Gallery
Peppermints in the Parlor
Sparrows in the Scullery
The Twin in the Tavern

The Trouble With Miss Switch
Miss Switch to the Rescue

BARBARA BROOKS WALLACE

SECRET IN
❧ ST. ❧
SOMETHING

Aladdin Paperbacks

New York London Toronto Sydney Singapore

First Aladdin Paperbacks edition February 2003
Copyright © 2001 by Barbara Brooks Wallace

ALADDIN PAPERBACKS
An imprint of Simon & Schuster Children's Publishing Division
1230 Avenue of the Americas
New York, NY 10020

Also available in an Atheneum Books for Young Readers hardcover edition.
Designed by Sonia Chaghatzbanian
The text of this book was set in Bembo.

Printed in the United States of America
2 4 6 8 10 9 7 5 3 1

The Library of Congress has cataloged the hardcover edition as follows:
Wallace, Barbara Brooks, 1922–
p. cm.
Summary: Fleeing from a cruel stepfather, eleven-year-old Robin takes his baby
brother and finds shelter with street boys living in a church in a tenement area
of New York City.
ISBN 0-689-83464-0 (hc.)
[1. Homeless persons—Fiction. 2. Brothers—Fiction.] I. Title.
PZ7.W1547 Sc 2001
[Fic]—dc21 99-049711
ISBN 0-689-85601-6 (Aladdin pbk.)

⚜

*For my husband, Jim,
who lights up my life.*

⚜

CONTENTS

Chapter I

Robin

⚶

N ot a flicker of light from a gas lamp, nor even an oil lantern, lit the dank entryway of the tenement building. Nothing, that is, more than the chilling, early-evening light that had to force its way through the grimy sliver of cracked glass set in the door. One flight up the narrow, steep stairs, and Robin found himself swallowed by darkness. Suffocating darkness reeking with the collected smells of rotting wood, clammy stained walls, general filth, and cabbage soup, made by someone lucky enough to have afforded the cabbage to put in it.

To screw up his failing courage, Robin tried to suck in whatever air was available to him, only to have his pounding heart quickly pump it right back out of his thin chest. Nor did it help keep the icy knot forming in his stomach from drawing tighter and tighter.

Robin wondered if he would ever be anything less than terrified every time he had to climb these stairs, or the stairs of other buildings just like it. Same darkness. Same smells. Same misery and fear huddled behind every door in the building, especially fear of *him*. Fear of his knock on the door and what it meant.

Robin hated the thought of that almost more than he hated the dark hallway. Yet why would they need to be afraid of *him?* No one else was, certainly not the street boys, boys whose homes were anyplace they could find to sleep at night. Street boys had the uncanny ability to smell out the fact that under his clothes trembled a body as threatening as a pale chicken hanging in the butcher's window—a chicken so reduced to skin and bones it could well have been nearly dead before anyone came along to wring its neck. Why then should the people behind the doors not be able to recognize that this puny, barely-turned-eleven boy, who could have passed for nine, was as frightened as they were?

But in the end, Robin knew there was no way to change that. For he also knew they were not so much frightened of him as of the person who sent him. Of that person they would be deathly afraid. And had reason to be!

Creeping along the hallway, he found the first door. After a hesitant knock, he waited. The voices behind the door came to a sudden stop, now as dead as the air in the hallway. The silence dragged on, as if a long enough silence would drive him away. Timidly, he knocked again.

The door finally opened, and a man peered out. Coarse stubble on his face did nothing to disguise the deep hollows in his cheeks. A worn vest sagged on his gaunt form. The curiously blank expression in his eyes never changed as he opened the door wider.

"I'll get the rent money," he said in a flat voice. Then he turned and walked heavily across the room, disappearing into the dark, windowless closet that served as a bedroom.

Standing miserably uncomfortable outside the doorway, Robin could see the entire meagerly furnished room. Intended for no more than one or two human beings, it was where seven lived, eight counting the baby asleep on a pile of rags in the corner, watched over by a small girl.

The narrow windows let in whatever fading light they could steal from the airless space not more than an arm's length away from the neighboring tenement building. It fell on a woman with her head bent low over a table barely lit by a small oil lamp, where she was at work beading ladies' slippers. An old woman and two young girls sat with her, sorting the beads she needed. Even the little boy sitting with them was at work, pasting paper onto cardboard candy boxes.

No one in the room looked up at Robin except the girl tending the baby. She stared at him curiously, but at a warning glance from her mother, quickly returned her attention to the baby.

The man soon came back. "Here," he said thrusting some coins and a paper bill into Robin's hand. "You don't have to count it. I can tell you it's . . . it's fifty cents short. You just tell him please, I know it's short." The man hesitated. His thin, veined hands began to twitch nervously at his sides. "My wife was . . . she had to see the doctor. . . ." He faltered and gave a hopeless shrug. "Tell him for sure next week he'll have it. Don't forget. Tell him Kringle said so."

Fifty cents short! Robin felt that all the air was suddenly squeezed from his chest. Fifty cents short! And *he* was the one who would have to tell Hawker Doak that a tenant was fifty cents short! Did Mr. Kringle think that this was a simple thing to do? Oh, surely he must have the money *some*place.

"But . . . but . . ." Robin stammered, "can't you . . . don't you . . ."

"You tell him Kringle said so," Mr. Kringle interrupted quickly. "Tell him Kringle makes a promise. All right?" He made an attempt at a smile. But his hands were twitching nervously at his side, and Robin could see that he was frightened, because he truly did not have the money someplace—or *any*place.

"I will. I'll . . . I'll tell him, Mr. Kringle," Robin said, shoving the money into an inside pocket of his jacket.

Mr. Kringle gave him only a brief nod, and then swiftly shut the door on him.

Fifty cents! Fifty cents! Fifty cents short! And Hawker Doak had warned him he had better not come in *one cent* short. Not one measly, miserable, murderous cent! One cent short and he would "get it," Hawker had said. So how many more welts and bruises on his chicken-skinny body would he, Robin, earn for being *fifty* cents short? Fifty cents already, and he still had seven more doors to knock on.

What if one, or two, or even all of them came up short? And what if, after all, Mr. Kringle had withheld the money because there *was* actually only a runt of a boy at his door instead of Hawker Doak? And what if the others all felt the same?

But in his head, Robin once again saw the twitching hands, and the fear in the sunken eyes. No, Robin might have been standing there, but it was Hawker Doak Mr. Kringle had been seeing. And it would be that way with the rest.

But how far would Hawker go in paving Robin's way to king-dom come? How much more than fifty cents short would it take? Robin stood motionless in the hallway, too paralyzed by these thoughts to move. Then, with a shudder, he finally put a hand up against the clammy wall and began once again to feel his tortuous way through the dark building. Soon, all too soon, his questions would be answered.

Less than forty-five minutes later, he had finished making his calls on seven more wretched families, from the pale young couple with the sickly, wailing baby in an attic room barely large enough to turn around in, and with a window so small any light or air entering through it could only be called an accident, to the family of eight plus a boarder, who in their cellar rookery shared with rats and roaches their walls of scaly paint, floors of cold, damp dirt, and their oftimes diet of little more than stale bread and water.

But all of them had somehow managed to scrape together enough to pay their rent. Every last person. Every last cent. It had all been carefully, painstakingly counted out into Robin's hand. But there was still the missing fifty cents. And he still had to face Hawker and explain it. Face Hawker! Robin could almost feel the heavy hand striking his arm, or his back, or whatever other spot was most convenient. But as he was starting down the crumbling brick steps leading from the stoop outside the building, he stopped suddenly as an idea came to him. There might be a way he could put off the reckoning for the time being, perhaps even until Mr. Kringle could make good his promise to pay the rent!

Although Hawker had never said so outright, Robin knew that he was being trained to do one of Hawker's jobs for him so Hawker could spend more time at one of the hundreds of establishments that served the refreshments he was partial to. Now, if he had indulged himself in enough of these refreshments, might he not be too befuddled to make a proper accounting of money handed to him? He had ordered Robin to meet him at The Whole Hog, five blocks away. This was not very far, and Robin could get there quickly. Too quickly. He needed to give Hawker as much time as possible to enjoy himself. This, unfortunately, meant staying holed up in the dismal building doing nothing but waiting in the dark as the minutes crawled by. Or he could take to the street as he would have done anyway, killing time by dragging his feet and dawdling about until he thought it was safe to reach his destination. And that is what he decided to do.

First, however, he pulled from his jacket pocket the old nickel pocket watch that had belonged to his papa, which he had so far managed to keep safely hidden from Hawker. After consulting it and determining that he should allow Hawker at least another half hour at The Whole Hog, Robin climbed down the remaining steps.

Streetlamps were already being lit. His mama had never allowed him out alone to roam the street at this hour. Mama! What he would not give now to hear her voice scolding him once again! But he would never hear that voice on this side of the grave, for she was no more. Suddenly, to his horror, he felt his eyes flood with tears.

But he quickly dashed the tears away with the sleeve of his patched, too-large jacket. Patched because it had once belonged to another boy. Too large because he could grow into it, and it would thus last longer. How Robin regretted complaining about both these points after his mama had scraped together enough money to buy him the jacket. It would, after all, probably be a very long time before Hawker would see fit to buy him another. Further, Robin had the faint hope now that a patched, oversized jacket was making him look a little more like one of the street boys he so feared. He had yet to put it to the test, as the familiar boys had not been around lately. But if they appeared, perhaps they would leave him alone. He wondered if he could even adopt the swagger so many of them had.

But no jacket in the world would do any good if he were caught with tears. Any street boy worth his salt would spot them in a flash, just as they always seemed to know when someone was a ripe subject for tormenting and teasing. Robin had been the victim often enough of a particular gang when he walked to school, a place whose insides that group had probably rarely seen, if ever.

He gave his eyes another fierce swipe with his sleeve. Then, pulling his cap down over his ears, thrusting his hands deep into his pockets, and hunching up inside his jacket, he attempted a swagger as he set out to somehow kill a half hour without being killed himself.

Actually, it was easy to melt into a street teeming with people who, unless a boy ran into one of them, had no more interest in him than if he were a rag dangling from a ragmonger's cart. Less. Why would anyone notice him when there were hundreds of children roaming the tenement streets? Robin had one heart-stopping moment, however, when he saw a gang of street boys headed right toward him. But they were not ones he recognized, and they looked through him as if he were nothing but a lamppost. Possibly because they were looking for a pocket to pick, and Robin was only a boy in a patched jacket, not a very likely prospect. Nonetheless, inside his pocket, Robin's fingers tightened around his nickel watch.

Beyond that, there were a great many other things happening on the street to keep his mind away from his forthcoming dreaded encounter with Hawker. For he was overwhelmed by the bedlam of confusion and racket swirling around him. Rickety wagons clogged the street, their loud-mouthed owners vying for space. Rusty wheels squealed and horses snorted. Housewives haggled with street vendors over the prices of rags and wilted vegetables. Newsboys shouted the headlines of evening papers.

To escape as much of this as he could, Robin hugged the walls, trying to interest himself in what lay behind the shop windows. At the fishmonger's he stared into the eyes of dead fish to which the word "fresh" had long since ceased to apply. At the butcher shop he gazed at ugly slabs of meat being enjoyed by something that might have been flies, only this was still winter and not the time for flies.

Some shops were not so deadly. One in particular had a sign in its dusty windows saying "buy or sell." It was filled with everything from trays of tarnished spoons, cheap rings, bracelets, and watches, to ladies' tortoiseshell hair combs. There were even two violins with broken strings hanging on the walls. Over the door of this shop he read the word "Pawnshop." Then his eyes fell on a large clock hanging on the pawnshop wall, its pendulum swinging. Could that be the right time?

Quickly he pulled his watch from his pocket, very careful to let no one see it. For someone in that crowd could snatch it from him, or just as easily accuse him of being a pickpocket. After all, how could a boy in a patched jacket be the owner of such a fine watch? And nickel though it might be, to Robin it was the finest watch in the world. But now this fine watch of his told him that he had managed to pass all but five minutes of the half hour he had set himself, and he must now hurry to face Hawker.

Breathless, he arrived in only four minutes at a disreputable brick building that seemed to be held up on either side by two equally disreputable buildings. But it looked like thousands of its kind even to the door, blackened and stained by filth from the city streets, splintered by the countless pairs of heavy boots that had kicked it in order to hasten their owner's entrance into the building's miserable interior. The only thing that distinguished this building from the rest was the sign hanging tipsily beside it. Portrayed on one side in paint that might once have been gold was a pig's snout. Across from the snout was the opposite end of the pig. Or might have been if so much of the curly tail had not been worn away. These two pig parts were joined by words barely legible that announced the building as being The Whole Hog. This was the place where Hawker was waiting for Robin. His heart starting to pound, he pushed open the door. . . .

And was hit in the face with the terrible stench of stale air, stale drink, and stale smoke, in a squalid room not large enough for half the bodies packed into it. In the murky light, men in work clothes and a few frowzy women sat crowded together, leaning heavily on an array of dark, scarred, wood tables. Some occupants had gone beyond simple leaning, and had collapsed on the table, arms sprawled out over their heads. No one, including the management, paid any attention to Robin as he huddled against the front wall, his eyes searching the room.

At first he saw only the dark knit cap on a head bent over a table, a cap like many others there, but he knew the black jacket under it at once. Oh, how well he knew it, for it was rarely off its owner. Sometimes it stayed on all night when he stumbled in late and fell into bed like a stone. The drooping head was a good sign, because it meant Robin had gauged his time just right. Under that cap would be a brain too befuddled to count money. But then the head rose.

There was the familiar red rag that served as a scarf tied around the neck. There was the thick black beard covering all the face but for the gash cutting across the cheek bone. There was the pitted nose over the thick, wet lips. And there were the dark eyes suddenly piercing Robin with a razor-sharp stare as the heavy lids narrowed around them.

"Get over here, boy!" Hawker Doak snarled. "You're late!"

Chapter II

OUT!

⚜

Shoving his chair away from the table where he had been slouching with two other men, Hawker hoisted himself up. But he never for a moment took his glaring eyes off Robin squeezing between tables and chairs as he made his way across the foul room. The moment he arrived, Hawker grabbed him roughly by the collar.

"This boy and I got private business," Hawker muttered under his breath to his tablemates.

"You comin' back?" one of the men asked. "Want we should save your seat?"

"Sure I'm comin' back, you dolt," Hawker growled. "What do you think? Just goin' over to the cubby at the back where everyone can't be stickin' their noses into what's none o' their affair."

Giving Robin a violent jerk that almost knocked him off his feet, Hawker dragged him away from the table, forcing a way to the back of the room to what was little more than a dent in the wall. It was large enough, however, for him to shove Robin in, and then plant himself in front so nothing but his huge, hulking back could be see by the rest of the room. Then he shot out a beefy hand at Robin.

"All right, boy, turn it over. Let's see what you did."

His hands shaking so hard he could hardly unbutton his jacket,

Robin dug into an inside pocket and started pulling out the money he had collected. But any lingering hope he had that the darkness of the hole in the wall where he stood would confuse Hawker was soon ended. His thick fingers were nimble as they counted every cent and crumpled dollar bill.

"Is this all?" he snapped. "Look at me, boy. I'm askin', is this all?"

Eyes glued to Hawker's accusing face, Robin nodded.

Hawker's eyebrows raised suspiciously. "You didn't by any chance lift a mite for yourself, did you? In another way of puttin' it, you didn't steal any, did you?" His eyes bored into Robin as he jammed the money inside his jacket.

"No," he said, answering his own question. "A scrawny little weasel like you wouldn't have the stomach for nothin' like that. But then why, I'm askin' you, are we comin' up fifty cents short? Who, I'm askin' you, didn't pay up? If you don't got a hole in your pocket, and you didn't steal it, who, I'm askin' you again, boy, who didn't pay up?"

"It . . . it . . . it was Mr. Kringle," Robin stammered. "He . . . he didn't have enough money to pay it all."

Hawker snorted. "Well, if that's what he told you, *I'm* tellin' you he's lyin'."

"But . . . but he said his wife had to see the doctor," Robin said. "He . . . he . . ."

"He nothin'!" Hawker snarled. "If you believe that, you believe Christmas comes twice a year, boy. She sits around earnin' money makin' them fancy slippers, don't she?"

"But he said to tell you he'd have the money next week," Robin said. "He said to tell you, 'Mr. Kringle makes a promise.'"

Hawker sneered. "Oh, he said that, did he? So what makes him think that him who owns the building is gonna like it if all I bring him is bloody promises? It's my neck or Kringle's is what it is. So you just tell him Hawker Doak makes a promise to *him*. He pays up now, or else he and his slipper-makin' missus, the old lady, and all their brats are *out*. You hear me, boy? Out! Now, I'm goin' back to my seat what's bein' held for me. You march right back to Kringle, and don't come back without the fifty cents. You understand me, boy?"

Even as Robin was nodding, Hawker grabbed him by the jacket collar once again and yanked him back to the table. "All right, get movin'! I'll be right here waitin' for you."

Oh yes, there was little doubt about *that*. Where the doubt lay was in whether Robin could come back with the fifty cents. And as he finally left The Whole Hog, one terrible word kept drumming in his head. Out! Out where? Where could the Kringle family go if they were put out? The street? Or perhaps a rat hole worse than the one they were in, if they were lucky enough to find one?

Robin remembered once when work at the docks had been slow for his papa, and he and Mama had gone around with worried looks. They had something "put aside" for such an event, they said, but was it enough? They had even breathed the word "out." How frightening it would be for someone to be put out. Of course, though they lived in the tenements, it was in a decent building, nothing so murderous as the one where Robin had been sent to collect rents. But out was out, no matter from what kind of building.

As Robin left The Whole Hog, he thought of the twitching hands by Mr. Kringle's sides, and the fear in his eyes. He thought of the thin, wasted face of the wife bent over the table, the shrunken, shrivelled grandmother, the pasty-faced children—all of them relentlessly slaving away over the beads and the boxes. Out! And they *would* be put out, too. For Robin believed Mr. Kringle truly did not have the fifty cents. So what was the use of knocking on that door again? Robin could not even bring himself to try.

But what then *was* he to do? Hawker had warned him not to come back without the fifty cents. Well, he did not have the fifty cents, and he had no way to get it. Or did he? What of his papa's valuable nickel watch and that pawnshop he had passed? Robin could not bear the thought of parting with his precious watch, but the pawnshop sign had clearly said, "Buy or Sell." So when Mr. Kringle paid the fifty cents he owed the following week, Robin would simply buy the watch back. He knew he would get at least fifty cents for it, probably a great deal more for a watch as splendid as this one, even if it was nickel and not solid gold or silver.

Robin started to walk quickly back in the direction from which he had just come. As night had now definitely fallen, he could only hope the pawnshop was still open. But it must be, for the streets were still teeming with people conducting business under the gaslights as if it were broad daylight.

When he arrived at the pawnshop, he saw through the window that the shop was still dimly lit inside. A man stood behind the counter reading a newspaper by the light of a small glass oil lamp. This was no doubt Nathaniel Slyke, proprietor, as noted on a small, worn sign attached to the window. For a few moments, Robin remained outside, afraid to go in. But through the dust in the window, Mr. Slyke in his shabby sweater looked dusty himself, bent and old and as harmless as one of the tarnished teaspoons left in trays in his shop to be sold. Robin timidly opened the door and entered.

Mr. Slyke's head instantly jerked up. No longer softened by the dust on the window, his face appeared sallow, with the sharp, cunning look of a fox. As soon as his eyes fell on Robin, they narrowed.

"What is it you want?" he asked abruptly. "Don't you touch anything in the trays, boy. If you want to look at something, just point it out, and I'll show it to you."

"I . . . I didn't come to buy anything," Robin said in a fading voice. "I have something to sell."

"Sell?" Mr. Slyke shrugged. "Well then, let's see what you have. Lay it on the counter."

Fumbling in his pocket as Mr. Slyke stared at him in silence,

Robin pulled out the watch and laid it down before him. Mr. Slyke picked it up and turned it in his hands, examining it closely.

"What did you want for it?" he asked indifferently.

Robin swallowed hard. "F-fifty cents, please."

"Fifty cents?" Mr. Slyke's eyebrows went up. "What did you think this watch was made of?"

"My papa said it was nickel . . . solid nickel," Robin replied with pride.

"Well, your papa should not have been telling you such lies," Mr. Slyke said. "This is nickel, all right, nickel *plate*. But I can give you twenty-five cents for it."

"T-twenty-five cents?" Robin repeated the words with disbelief. "Is . . . is that all?"

Mr. Slyke set the watch back down on the counter and pushed it toward Robin. With his other hand he picked up his newspaper, indicating that he intended to give no more of his time to the transaction. "Solid nickel watches don't go for much," he said, "but you can get nickel plate in the catalogue for ninety-eight cents. Who's going to buy a watch like this in a pawnshop for more than fifty? Twenty-five is all I can give you."

Twenty-five cents! What good would twenty-five cents do when Robin had to return to The Whole Hog with fifty? And for twenty-five cents, why leave his treasured watch in the custody of Mr. Slyke, where someone else might purchase it and Robin would never see it again? Hesitantly, he picked up the watch from the counter.

"I . . . I might just keep it for now," he said.

"You can take it down the street," Mr. Slyke said. "But I can tell you, they won't give you more than twenty cents. Still, do as you please."

"Th-thank you," said Robin.

Mr. Slyke's eyes dropped down to the newspaper as if he had no wish to continue the conversation. But as Robin trailed across the shop to the front door, he could feel Mr. Slyke's sharp eyes fastened on his back the whole way.

Robin started slowly off down the street, dragging his feet as if they had turned to lead. The pawnshop had been his only hope. Now what was he to do? He could still hear Hawker's warning, "Don't come back without the fifty cents." Well, Robin still had no fifty cents. All he could do was go home and await Hawker's arrival—and with it, no doubt, a new crop of welts and bruises. He would go home and—and—no! He would not sit there in fear and trembling awaiting the sound of Hawker's heavy boots on the stairs. Not at all!

Once again, his footsteps quickened. Faster and faster all the way to the building where he lived. It was not to await Hawker, however. It was to get something. Something he had stupidly forgotten had been there all along!

Chapter III

A Sad Explanation

⚓

"What kept you, boy?" snarled Hawker. "You been gone a long time."

Robin had to swallow the lump in his throat, but he was prepared with his story. He had been rehearsing it all the way to The Whole Hog just in case Hawker actually noticed how long the mission had taken.

"It's . . . it's what I told you," Robin said. "Mr. Kringle didn't have the money. But . . . but he went to get it someplace, and I had to wait for him to come back."

"So he had someplace to get it, did he? Why didn't he go get it in the first place?" Hawker growled. "They always have a place they can go get it, if they've a mind to do it. Well, boy, I hope you've learned a big lesson about rent collectin'. So all right, hand it over."

Fifty cents, it seemed, was not a large enough sum for Hawker to drag Robin to the cubby at the back for privacy. He took the coins Robin handed him, carelessly counted them, and stuffed them inside his jacket. His two friends, meanwhile, appeared to find this whole performance highly entertaining, for they sat glued to it, one of them slack jawed, the other with a half grin on his face.

"All right, show's over," Hawker said sourly. "You can go now, boy, and . . ."

"Hey, not so quick, Hawker! How about you interdooce us to this boy o' yours," the slack-jawed individual broke in, leering at

Robin with squint eyes that seemed to look in two directions at the same time. These were lodged on either side of a flat red nose as lumpy as a meat pie. It was attached to an equally red face bulging out from a cap so greasy it was no longer any nameable color.

"Looks like now we'll be seein' more o' him, one way or t' other, and you never know when us bein' familiar with him might come in handy. Don't you agree with my line o' thinkin', Quill?"

"Maggot's got a point," his tablemate replied in a thready voice that sounded as if it were being pulled through a keyhole. This man was as narrow as the other was broad. A narrow face, a narrow nose, crafty narrow eyes, a frame so narrow he could have fitted into a crack in a wall and disappeared so quickly he would leave nothing behind but an evil whisper of air.

"I don't see how either one o' you got any point," grumped Hawker. "But first o' all, don't go bleatin' about him bein' any boy o' mine. I inherited him, more's the rotten luck."

"Seems to me as you're makin' good use o' your rotten luck," said Quill with a crooked grin.

"And you knowed about him b'fore you married his ma," Maggot said. "You can't go cryin' about it, Hawker. Anyways, maybe it'll learn you not to be wantin' so hard what ain't yours, mostly 'cause it ain't yours. This time you ended up getting' what you wanted. Now you gotta live with it."

"Maggot's got another point," Quill said agreeably.

"Aw, shut your big yaps, both o' you," Hawker said, clenching his fists angrily.

"Now, you don't need to go makin' fists over us offerin' some words o' friendly advice," said Maggot. "You're too quick makin' them fists, Hawker. How many fights you got into over doin' it, mostly for nothin'? One day it's gonna be the end o' you when a knife does more'n just put a beauty mark on your cheeks."

"Well, I don't want to hear any more o' your points," groused Hawker.

"Here's one anyway, Hawker," said Quill. "You can't look for us to sit around bleedin' over your hard luck when you got this boy workin' for you. You ain't allowin' him back to school just so's he can go on the streets sellin' papers. You're lookin' to puttin' him in a factory maybe. You already got him collectin' rents, and he learns fast. Look how he's brung you the missin' fifty cents, pretty as you please. Seems like you ain't wasted no time startin' to train him. So what's to bleed about?"

"What do you mean, 'wasted no time'?" Hawker snapped. "Didn't I give him a whole week to do all the snivelin' he wanted after his ma died?"

"Got to say that was generous o' you, Hawker," said Maggot. "And o' course, there's that other little matter you got stuck with. Can't blame you for bein' sore 'bout that. You knew 'bout it like-wise b'fore you got hitched, but got to admit I'm willin' to bleed a little for you 'bout that one."

"Well," said Quill, "you can just farm it out like you're doin'. If it lives long enough, you'll have two workin' for you, protectin' your old age. Anyways, no use talkin' 'bout it, right, Hawker?"

"Right!" said Hawker, scowling.

"So what's this boy's name?" Quill asked. "Ain't you gonna tell us?"

Hawker jerked his head at Robin. "Tell 'em your name, boy. Don't just stand there like a tree stump."

Robin, who had been listening to the conversation being held on his bleak future as if he were, in truth, a tree stump with no ears and certainly no feelings, could barely get out his name.

"It's . . . it's Robin," he said weakly.

Upon hearing this, both Quill and Maggot grinned. "Don't blame you for not wantin' to use it," Maggot said. "What kind o' name is that for a boy?"

Hawker shook his head in disgust. "His ma said when she was havin' him, this bird came up to the window and was talkin' to her. That's the kind o' bird it was, so she named the baby after it."

"Sounds like his ma was a pretty face with no brain behind it," said Maggot. "Wonder his pa never said nothin' to stop it."

"Maybe where the family come from, it ain't so strange," said Quill. "Seems to me somewheres I heard o' boys named it."

"Not around here," grumbled Hawker.

"Well, when he gets out on the street, maybe he'll start callin' hisself somethin' else, just for protection," said Maggot.

"And speakin' o' street," said Hawker, "you better go hit the street, boy, and pick up the brat. I ain't aimin' to pay Mrs. Jiggs any more than I got to. Now get a move on!"

As Robin hurried down the street, he had to keep dashing away the angry tears from his eyes. Never mind that the street boys might see him. Never mind that some of the streets he had to travel were dark and very nearly deserted, streets that might ordinarily have filled him with fright. All he knew was that his brain was pounding with rage.

How dared those men talk about his mama as they had? A pretty face with no brain behind it! Well, *they* were hideously *ugly* faces with not a single brain to share between the two of them! How he would have loved to hurl *that* insult at them! And he would have if he were ten feet tall, with muscles bulging on his arms—a raging bull instead of a chicken-skinny boy. He would have flattened them on the ground right there at The Whole Hog. Then he would stomp on them until they begged for mercy.

As for Hawker, simply throwing him to the ground and kicking him was too good for him. Robin, the raging bull, would ram him and ram him until he was nothing but a bloody pulp. Tearing his eyes out might also be considered. Anything that would make him howl with pain and beg Robin's forgiveness. For after all, it was because of what Hawker had told them that made the men say the things they had. Hawker wanting what he could not have, and when he got it, having to "live with it." Where could that have come from but Hawker himself? It was if winning Mama after Papa died was a punishment for having wanted her in the first place.

Hawker seemed to have been captivated by her from the very beginning. From the time he had met Robin's papa at the docks where they both worked and been invited to visit the family in their home. Papa enjoyed it when anyone was taken with his pretty wife, for he was proud of her sparkling smile and dancing green eyes. He liked having them admired. And how different Hawker was back then when he had come calling. For all his roughness, he was a gentleman, Mama and Papa both felt. But it was all put on, as she was to learn to her sorrow.

Why had Mama ever married Hawker Doak? Why? Actually Robin needed no one to give him the answer, for like it or not, he already knew it. For his mama had told him.

Late one night, after he and Mama had had a taste of Hawker's violence, and Hawker was snoring in bed, Robin had awakened to hear the sound of someone sobbing softly in the kitchen. Creeping from his cot in the tiny room next to it, he had found Mama at the kitchen table with her head buried in her arms. Robin had quietly sat down beside her and put a hand over hers. Then, at long last, he had asked the question that he always believed was not for him, a young boy, to ask.

"Mama, why did you marry him?"

She looked up at him, the cold moonlight that came through the window glistening on her tear-stained cheeks. "Oh, Robin, I always thought you understood why. You must remember how terrible it was for us when your papa was so suddenly taken from us by that cruel accident at the docks?"

"I do remember!" Robin had replied earnestly. For how could he ever forget what, until that time, had been the worst memory of his life?

"Well, then," she continued, "you must also think of how it was for me to lose him, and at the same time to realize I was left alone to take care of not only you, but of the infant I had just learned was to come. I knew I could never earn enough from the sewing I take in, so I would have had to go into the factories. The baby would have to be farmed out, and you would be left on your own all day."

"I could have worked," Robin had said. "I could have given up school."

"Never! Your papa was never more than a dock worker, in London as well as here. We took what little we had to cross the ocean, hoping to find a better life someday. But when your papa was a lad, he had his schooling," Mama had said proudly. "And when I was a lass, so did I. Never would I let you give that up. So going into the factories was what it was to be for me. And then Hawker asked me to marry him. Right away, he said, so all would believe the baby was his when it came.

"I think he feared he might lose me to someone else, if you can believe it," she added with a sad smile. "But he seemed a good man, Robin. I had no call to think otherwise. Then soon after, I didn't look as good to him as when I belonged to someone else, and he turned into what I believe he always had been, a cruel and hard man. And now do you understand it all?"

"Yes, Mama," Robin had said. "But he *never* cared for me, even when he came visiting you and Papa. I knew from his eyes. And you know how when I tried calling him 'Pa,' as you asked me to do, he hit me across the mouth. And you see how he hits me all the time."

"I know," she replied. "I've been afraid to say anything for fear he would treat you even worse. He has threatened me as well, and some day I know he will make good his threats. The very thought of him frightens me, Robin, especially now."

"Why especially now?" Robin had asked, scared by the look on her face.

"Because of something I must tell you," she replied. "I've put it off, but I fear I can put it off no longer."

And what Robin learned was that, even though he already

knew she had been ailing even before the baby came, the doctor had now told her she had little time left in this world. It was why, she said, she had been showing Robin how to care for the baby. She had pleaded with Hawker to let Robin continue in school and help her when he came home, though Hawker had wanted to send him to work. She had thought so far ahead as to hide for him the few coins she could save, carefully laying them flat under the linoleum that lined the kitchen cupboard. That, in truth, was where he had found the fifty cents.

"Robin," Mama had said at last, "you are young to have this burden, but you must promise me to do all you can do to protect the baby from Hawker. But oh, Robin, I fear for you both!"

Mama soon to be no more! It could not be! But it was. For very soon afterward, she was gone, and the worst memory of Robin's life had now been replaced with one even worse. Hawker, as he had told his friends at The Whole Hog had, out of the kindness of his heart, allowed Robin a whole week to do "all the snivelin" he wanted.

But that week was over, and Robin no longer went to school. Yet what could he do about it?

Nothing!

He would no doubt have to lie about his age and be sent to work in a factory. And what could he do about *that*?

Nothing!

And what of his baby brother? Poor little Danny! Not quite four months old with a terrible future already mapped out for him. And if, after being farmed out to such a place as that run by Mrs. Jiggs, he even grew up at all, would he be like Hawker, the only papa he was ever to know? It was an unbearable thought.

Robin had promised Mama he would do everything in his power to keep his little brother safe. But deep in her heart, she must have known there was nothing he could do to save Danny, or himself, from Hawker Doak.

Nothing!

Chapter IV

Escape!
⫪

Robin woke with a start, only to have his blood instantly turn to ice. For what had awakened him was the sound of Danny crying, and Hawker yelling.

"Shut up! Shut up, you little brat!"

Robin leaped from his cot. By the light of an oil lamp making its feeble way from the kitchen, he saw Hawker's huge, threatening form leaning over Danny's little crib. His hand was raised as if to strike.

If Robin had hesitated a moment to think, he might have been too paralzyed with fear to move. Instead, he ducked under Hawker's arm and grabbed Danny up.

"I'll take care of him, Hawker. I'll make him stop crying."

Hawker, instead of lowering his arm, must have felt it necessary to make the raising of it worthwhile. He laid a bruising clout on Robin's back. If the crib had not been there to catch him, Robin would have hit the floor, taking Danny with him.

"That's for remindin' you you should o' taken care o' the job before I got home," Hawker snarled. "I don't like comin' in to find a bawlin' brat waitin' for me. Now you get him quiet in a hurry, or you get him out o' here and keep him out 'til he shuts up. You got that, boy?"

"Y-yes, Hawker," Robin said, knowing as he bounced Danny

in his arms to quiet him that it was probably Hawker himself who had awakened Danny when he came crashing into the apartment in his usual manner.

Hawker started to leave, then hesitated and turned back. "And you might as well know I'm takin' back collectin' the rents. You're not to do newspapers neither. A little weasel like you wouldn't last thirty minutes on the streets, nor bring in enough to pay Mrs. Jiggs to keep the brat while you're there. So tomorrow, boy, you ain't eleven any more. You turn fourteen, and we visit a factory or two, and see who pays the best, or who'll even take you. Now, I'm hittin' my bed and you see I don't get woke again, boy!"

He stumped noisily to his room, and in a few moments, Robin heard the springs squeal as he fell into bed. In no time, snores were rumbling through the apartment.

Robin, in the meantime, quickly pulled Danny's half-full bottle of milk from where it sat in the window box outside to keep it cold and then warmed it at the sink. The milk soon put Danny back to sleep.

Robin climbed wearily back into his cot. But he had no sooner laid down and closed his eyes than they flew open again, and he lay staring into the darkness, filled with dread. He had been so frightened when standing by Hawker and praying that Danny would quiet down, he had barely heard all that Hawker had to say. Now the crushing words came back to him. "Tomorrow you ain't eleven any more. You turn fourteen, and we visit a factory."

Robin knew that a child who could read and write need only be fourteen to be allowed to work in a factory. That a puny eleven-year-old could pass for fourteen was laughable. But Robin also knew that many children lied, or their parents lied for them, to get into the factories. And many factory owners or foremen accepted the lies. Hawker would lie, and expect Robin to lie. He knew that if he confessed to his true age, he could start numbering the days he had remaining in this world.

And what of Danny? Poor helpless little Danny. He would be spending his days in that pigsty run by Mrs. Jiggs. No, worse than a pigsty, for a pigsty was probably better kept than her baby farm. Robin could not bear the thought of what he had seen when he went to pick up Danny that evening.

He could not at one glance count the number of babies crawling around, dirty diapers dangling about their legs, faces filthy with caked cereal and milk, most of them sobbing piteously. Mrs. Jiggs herself, a slatternly woman of mountainous proportions, sat squeezed into a rocking chair, raising to her lips a tin cup giving off fumes bespeaking the same kind of liquid refreshment that perfumed such places as The Whole Hog. Unable, or simply too lazy, to get to the door when Robin had knocked, she had yelled at him to come in.

"You can look for him over there, dearie," she had said to his request for Danny. She waved her arm in the direction of a pile of dirty rags in a corner of the room.

And there Robin had found Danny, his face scarlet from screaming away unattended, along with the other screaming babies. Robin could hardly get him away from Mrs. Jiggs' establishment fast enough. And that, of course, was where Danny would be doomed to spend the better part of whatever growing years might be left him.

But a more horrifying memory than that was of Hawker's big, beefy hand raised threateningly over Danny's crib, with little mistaking where it was destined to come down. Robin had felt that hand on various parts of himself, and knew the strength and anger behind it. If he had not snatched Danny up, would the hand have come down on him in the same manner? How many times could a tiny baby survive such blows as that?

Robin stared into the darkness, seeing again and again the picture of Hawker's hand coming down over Danny's crib. And then slowly, as if he were a wind-up toy unable to stop moving once its key had been turned, Robin pulled aside his blanket, put one leg, and then the other onto the floor. Finding his clothes in the dark, he dressed himself, but was careful to leave off his shoes. In his stockinged feet, he padded softly into the kitchen and lit a candle, setting it on the windowsill in the farthest corner. Lifting down from a peg in the wall the cloth shopping bag his mama had made for herself, he set it on the kitchen table.

Then he crept back into his and Danny's room, where he gathered all the diapers he could find, Danny's shirts and two little worn sweaters, once Robin's. Back in the kitchen, he carefully wrapped Danny's four clean baby bottles in the diapers, as well as two he filled with milk and teaspoonfuls of sugar syrup, a tiny tin spoon and a tin bowl, a paper sack of cereal, and a bottle of sugar syrup. All of these, together with the shirts and sweaters, Robin packed in the shopping bag.

This done, he cautiously slid a chair over to the cupboard and climbed onto it. Pushing aside a small stack of dishes, he lifted up the linoleum liner, and one by one picked up the coins under it, laying them on the counter. Then he replaced the linoleum and pushed back the dishes.

The next thing he did was put on his patched jacket, and put the coins into the inside pocket where he had carried the rent money. Then what he did was enter the dark room where Hawker lay snoring. Crossing over to the chest of drawers, he reached behind the mirror for a key, and with it unlocked and opened one top drawer. It was a drawer Hawker allowed no one to open except himself. But Robin's mama had had a very good idea of what was in it. And so did Robin.

For Hawker, part-time dock worker, part-time rent collector for landlords, was also a part-time dealer in stolen goods, jewelry not excepted. But it almost seemed as if he kept little or no accounting of what he had in that department. For often when he entered the apartment on unsteady legs, he would simply toss one thing or another carelessly into the drawer. On several occasions, he had even left a pin or two, several rings, or a string of beads on a table for anyone to see.

Now, in the dark, Robin dipped a hand into the drawer. But even in his curiously dreamlike state, he knew that he should not raise Hawker's suspicion that the drawer has been raided. So he took only the two things his fingers encountered, a pin and something small, flat, and round attached to a chain. Thrusting both of these into his jacket pocket, he closed and locked the drawer, hung the key back behind the mirror, and padded from the room.

Next, he gathered up the shopping bag and his shoes, then quietly opened the front door and laid the bag and shoes on the floor just outside it. Now, at last, after stuffing two candles and a box of matches into his pocket, he pulled on his cap, which hung on a kitchen peg, and went to fetch Danny.

It was then Robin realized he could not risk waking Danny by trying to put on his bonnet and cape, so he stuffed the bonnet into his own pocket and threw the cape over his own shoulder. Then, praying as hard as he had ever prayed in his life, he wrapped Danny's blanket around him, leaving only a small space for his face to peek through, and gently lifted him from the crib. Danny, now pleasantly filled with milk, stayed sound asleep.

After snuffing the candle burning in the kitchen, Robin was guided to the front door by the dim light of a wall lamp that flickered all night in the hallway of the building. After closing the door, he carefully laid Danny on the floor while he packed the cape into the shopping bag and kneeled to pull on and tie his shoes. Then he picked up Danny, snugly wrapped in his blanket cocoon, and the shopping bag, and crept from the building.

Until then, Robin had been moving as if he were in a trance, as if he were, in truth, a wind-up toy, as if someone else inside him were giving him orders that he was simply obeying. Was he only dreaming? None of what he had just done even seemed real to him.

But when the cold night air struck his face, the spell was broken. He was shocked into realizing that he had been so intent on the escape from Hawker, he had given no thought as to what to do after the escape. Now here he was in the street with his tiny baby brother, and he had no idea where to go, or what to do next. Not a single idea in the whole world!

Chapter V

A Desperate Measure

Pressing Danny more closely to himself to guard against a chill-ing wind, Robin huddled in the doorway of the building, beginning to wonder if he had gone mad. What had he been think-ing, doing this? Should he not turn right around and go back, and take his chances that things might not be as bad as he thought?

Oh yes, why not wait and see if Danny could survive the ten-der care of Mrs. Jiggs? Why not see if he could survive one or two blows from Hawker's gentle hand? Finally, why not wait and see if Robin himself could survive that same hand, or a factory, and stay alive long enough to protect his little brother, as he had promised he would do?

No! No! No! He really would be mad, raging mad, to go back into that building. How could he and Danny end up anything but dead, and have to suffer torture into the bargain? Better if they died on the streets, quickly—and together.

But Robin was not ready to die. Not just yet. Not now, when he had taken the daring first step in rescuing Danny and himself from Hawker Doak. But the second step would be far more diffi-cult, and more perilous, as he now realized. For, though packing himself and Danny up to leave was perilous enough, what with Hawker asleep in the very next room, it had been done in a place Robin had known from the time he was a small boy. Now what he must do did not include a candle shedding its friendly little light on a familiar kitchen. This second step was to be more like stepping off a cliff into total darkness, not knowing where he and Danny would land or, if they survived the fall, what they would do when they landed. But it was a risk he was now determined to take.

The wind seemed to bite right through Robin's jacket. Goosebumps rose on his arms. He was cold. He was tired. And now he wished he had finished his supper of stale bread, or at least packed the tag end of the loaf into his pocket. He had been so intent on preparing Danny for the flight that he had managed to forget all about himself. Danny, however, well-wrapped in his warm blanket, was still happily fast asleep.

Robin knew he could not stand there forever, trying to stay protected from the wind. What if the unthinkable happened and Hawker awoke to discover them gone? He might actually be glad to be rid of them, yet more than likely he would be enraged at being made a fool of. That would be quite enough to send him after them.

But there was something else—that pin and the object on a chain now residing in Robin's jacket pocket. Why, Robin asked himself, had he taken those things? And what kind of harebrained idea was it anyway to go right into Hawker's room where he lay snoring? Robin decided he must truly have been in a trance, and it was only his mama and papa looking down from heaven that had protected him. Further, the things he had taken were of absolutely no use to him, for it was money he would need, and not a pin and a—a—what was that other—a locket? Robin's heart skipped a beat.

Mama had breathed a word that sounded like "locket" to him in the faintest whisper just before she died. But she had been too weak and too close to leaving this world to say more. Was this the locket she meant? Did it contain pictures of Mama and Papa? Thinking it was probably hidden from Hawker, Robin had searched desperately for it during the week he had been allowed to "snivel" over his mama. But he had found nothing.

Was it possible the locket he had accidentally pulled from Hawker's forbidden drawer was the one? Could Hawker have found it himself and tossed it in along with all his other stolen jewelry? No, it was probably too much to hope. Taking the pin and locket had simply turned Robin into a thief, and would so infuriate Hawker if he found out about it, he would do all in his power to find and punish the culprit. So no, indeed, Robin could not remain standing where he was if he valued his and Danny's lives.

The side street outside the building was deserted, silent but for an empty tin can caught by sudden gusts of wind that sent it clanking off down the sidewalk. The wind sent scraps of dirty paper fruitlessly chasing after it. As the moon was hidden behind scudding clouds, the only light now came from a solitary streetlamp flickering half a block away. Accompanied by the lonely, forlorn sound of the empty tin can, and only the blinking light ahead, Robin set out with his baby brother.

But Robin's bold spirits soon gave way to terror. For though the tenement streets were bad enough earlier—with their shoddy storefronts, their street booths and peddlers' carts and wagons selling rags and rotten fruits and vegetables, their street brawls and loud, noisy voices—at night they produced different kinds of horrors.

From countless establishments akin to The Whole Hog there poured streams of brutish men and frowzy women whose coarse laughter could turn to frightening shouts and curses at a moment's notice. Dark entries to alleys became darker and more sinister. Stairwells were gaping black holes where who knew what kind of tramps and thieves roosted, sharing night quarters with rats that came up from the sewers. Even the boarded-up windows of crumbling buildings were ominous, for who knew what terrible secrets they hid that might be unleashed on the unwary passerby. About the only horrors not present were the gangs of street boys. It was too late at night even for them, and they must have been already holed up in their dens under a pier by the river, in the back of a wagon parked for the night, or in a large, abandoned iron pipe. Some might even be in the stairwells, if they had been lucky enough to lay claim to them before any other night life moved in.

Absence of street boys aside, Robin's terror seemed to grow until his courage had almost evaporated entirely. Again and again he was tempted to turn back. And why not? For all he knew, he might be exchanging a familiar horror for an unfamiliar one that could be far worse. But he could never erase the picture of that cruel hand raised against Danny. So with his heart in his throat, Robin scurried past the dark, threatening alleys and stairwells, and the boarded-up windows, and went on, trying to get as far away from Hawker as possible.

So far, however, he had not come up with a single idea as to where he should take Danny, or how they were to live. And now he was so tired his brain had shut down. He had heard of cheap lodging houses where for a few pennies he could have a place to lie down for the night. Perhaps in the morning he could think more clearly of what he should do. On the other hand, he had also heard how grim such places were. Like the dark, evil stairwells, they were the roosting places of the worst kind of tramps and thieves. Even if he dared to go into one of these places himself, he would not take Danny into one. Besides, he needed every penny of the two dollars and fifty cents he had in his pocket, that being the remainder of the three dollars his mama had left him after fifty cents had been given to Hawker.

Perhaps he should find the nearest police station, and throw himself on the mercy of the policemen, begging them to find a kind home for himself and Danny so they could stay together. Oh yes, a police station, where, classed as a runaway, Robin, along with Danny, would be back with Hawker Doak within the hour! Worse, what if the pin and locket were discovered in Robin's pocket? Danny would be tossed back into the arms of Hawker, and Robin himself would be tossed into the arms of a reformatory!

Everything else Robin came up with had the unhappy ending of seeing him separated from Danny forever. He had heard of something called the Foundling Asylum, a place that took in baby waifs, but not older children. And surely not a boy Robin's age. He had no idea of what happened to babies when they were infants, but once Danny disappeared through their doors, Robin was certain he would never see his little brother again.

On the night Robin had had the long, tearful talk with his mama, she had said that perhaps she should leave Danny in a basket on the doorstep of a big church attended by the wealthy, where he might be taken by some loving family. But, of course, Robin knew she could never have brought herself to take such a desperate measure. Nor had Robin considered it. At least not until this very moment, when he started to think about it.

Church! A big, handsome church attended by the wealthy! What if Robin were to find one and leave Danny on its front step? Who would not want him, this baby with the most beautiful blue eyes in the world, and a cap of soft golden ringlets? And Robin would leave the shopping bag with his cape, his bonnet, his baby bottles, his little tin spoon and bowl, *and* the two dollars and fifty cents, so his new family could know that this was a baby who had been cared for and loved.

But, and this was an enormous BUT, the big difference would be that Robin himself would be hiding behind a bush, or a church pillar, or even loitering about across the street, and would see who took Danny! Such wealthy people as would be attending the church would surely own a carriage, and Robin would simply take note of the number of that carriage. This clever trick would help him to find the people. After a day or two had passed—ample time, he felt, for them to fall so in love with Danny they would never wish to part with him—Robin would present himself to them as Danny's brother.

If he were lucky, they might even take him as well, not wishing to see them separated. If not so lucky, they perhaps might allow him to visit Danny from time to time. At least then they would not be lost to one another forever.

However, one problem remained. How was Robin himself to survive? Though he would hate doing it, perhaps he should keep out fifty or seventy-five cents from the two dollars and fifty cents. That would buy him several nights at a cheap lodging house until he found a way to earn money. Perhaps he could become a newsboy after all. But he was too tired to think about it now. All he wanted to think about was putting the tenements far behind himself, and finding the proper church. His steps quickened.

"Where do you think you're goin' in such a hurry, my lad?" said a gruff voice, coming at Robin out of the darkness.

Robin froze in his steps. He turned slowly around and found himself looking up into the stern, scowling face of a policeman!

"I . . . I . . . I . . ." Robin stammered.

"Cat got your tongue, eh?" said the policeman. "Well then, maybe you can do better with this next question. What you got in that bundle you're carryin', and that bag?"

"It's . . . it's . . . my baby brother," quavered Robin. "And his food and clothes are in the bag."

"Will you be kind enough to step over here under the lamp and let me have look?" inquired the policeman, still stony-faced.

Robin, his legs turned to rubber, quickly moved over to the lamp, and pulled back the corner of blanket around Danny's face.

The policeman peered down. His face instantly softened. "Why, so it is!" he whispered. "And bless me, he's fast asleep. Now, step back away from the light, lad. We don't want to waken him, do we? Oh, I'm Officer Bugle, by the by."

Robin gratefully stepped back into the darkness, though his heart continued to pump at a great high rate.

"But you have to tell me where it is you're goin' at this late hour, and takin' a baby with you," Officer Bugle said in a kindly voice.

For a frightening moment, Robin's brain stopped working. But then he heard himself saying, "My pa is sick, and the baby was crying and keeping him awake. So my mama told me to take him over to my aunt's. That's where I'm going now."

Officer Bugle shook his head with a look showing his view of such an order. "And who is the aunt, and where might she live, lad?" he asked. "It's safer for you if you let me know that."

"It's . . . it's Mrs. Kringle," said Robin, and then proceeded to give the address of the building where he had collected rents earlier that day.

Again Officer Bugle shook his head. "One of those holes," he muttered under his breath. "But you see, it's a good thing you told me, lad, because you're goin' in just the wrong direction. You need to turn around and go back the other way."

"Oh, thank you, sir," said Robin. "I must have taken the wrong turn back there. But I know I can find it now. Thank you very much, Officer."

"No trouble at all," said Officer Bugle, smiling. "You're a good boy, and you've done a fine job gettin' that baby brother of yours back to sleep. Take care you don't wake him. Good night then, lad."

"Good night, sir," said Robin, watching Officer Bugle go on down the street, whistling, while he himself turned to go back in exactly the opposite direction from the one he had been taking.

Oh, how much he would have liked to tell this nice man the truth. But the man was a policeman, and he would have had to do what was proper for a policeman to do, deposit Robin and Danny with Hawker. As it was, Robin was going to have to go all around the block to get back to where he would be heading in the right direction to find a church.

Church! What a fine place for Robin to be going. For in something less than two hours he had robbed someone and told a lie. He had suddenly become a thief and a liar. Perhaps that was what it took to survive on the street. If so, he was now well qualified. He only hoped his punishment would never be anything worse than having to go out of his way around the block!

Chapter VI

A Whole Nest!

𝕋

On and on Robin trudged. Then at last he saw it! The tenements had now been left behind, and there it was—rising tall and stately into the night—the church he was looking for!

Six gas lights on the street around it palely lit up its stone walls and stained-glass arched windows. Rising up from the walls was a lofty spire, now only a shadow against the night sky. At the foot of the church was a lawn lined with spreading junipers and clipped boxwood, all protected by a low, wrought iron fence. Through a large opening in the fence, a brick walk led from the street to the massive carved oak doors of the church.

This was just the church, Robin felt as he walked up the brick path with Danny. Surely among all those who came to this beautiful place there would be someone who would love to have him. Robin would just set him down gently on the steps now and—but no! What was he thinking? Leave Danny there the rest of the night? Even with himself curled up somewhere nearby in the bushes, this was about as harebrained an idea as helping himself to the jewelry in Hawker's precious drawer. More harebrained than that, if the truth be known. For in this case he might be risking Danny's life, or his safety at the very least.

What he needed to do, Robin decided, was find some out-of-the-way little cubby at the side or back of the church where he could curl up and have Danny right with him. It would be difficult to lay Danny on the front steps of the church in broad daylight, but somehow he would find a way to do it. Danny still in his arms, Robin left the steps and went around a big circle of yews and boxwoods at the corner of the church to make a search for the cubby. But there was not one to be found at the side of the church. He began to think he would find none at all, and would have to curl up with Danny under one of the bushes. But he would not consider that until he had first gone all around the building.

When he rounded the back corner of the church, he found himself in near-total darkness. The street lamps gave just enough light to reveal a pair of iron railings rising up over brick steps that led down to a cellar door. A cellar door that dipped in enough to provide a cubby for Robin and Danny!

But before Robin could take the first step down, he saw a pinprick of light flickering on the pane of a small cellar window halfway down the back of the church. Robin held his breath. Was there someone in there with an oil lamp or a candle? Might that someone be coming through the door? Would he be caught there with Danny? And then the pinprick of light disappeared, and the window became once more only a small square of black glass like all the other windows.

Robin was very, very tired by this time. His arms ached from carrying Danny. His legs ached from walking. And might not his brain be tired enough to be playing tricks on him? He stood watching the dark window for several minutes, and the light never came back. Nor, for that matter, did anyone come through the door.

Once again he started down the steps, and this time went all the way to the bottom of the stairwell. There he discovered it was colder than it had been at the top. No longer warmed by walking, he felt the cold digging all the way through his jacket into his bones. He began to shiver uncontrollably. And what of Danny? He was now snug and warm in his blanket cocoon, but would that cocoon be warm enough down in that stone well during the next few hours, the coldest time of the night?

Why, oh why, could they not be on the other side of that splintered old door? In a sudden burst of despair, Robin grabbed the door handle and began to rattle it, somehow pressing down on the latch as he did. And the door swung open.

Whether someone had forgotten to lock the door, or whether it always remained unlocked, made no difference to Robin. Whichever it was, it was some kind of miracle. He stepped through the doorway, and he and Danny were instantly wrapped in a blanket of warm air. A furnace was clearly at work someplace in the cellar. Yes, this was definitely a place where the two of them could spend the night. Robin closed the door behind him.

With the closing of the door, the pale light from the nearby street lamp was shut out, and the two were now plunged into total darkness. But Robin had seen doors when they came in, doors to rooms. A room was the safest place to be. If they remained in the hallway, they might be discovered in the morning. But how to find a room without first lighting a candle? To do that meant laying Danny down on the floor and risk waking him. Robin did not want to use one of his two precious bottles of milk to put Danny back to sleep, for they might be needed in the morning. Well, why not feel his way around the wall? Was that not what he had done that very morning when he was collecting rents? He was getting to be an old hand at it.

Feeling along the wall with one hand, he started down the hallway. He found a door almost immediately, but it was locked. So was the second. And third. So he went on. But the very next doorway was not only not locked, it was actually open. He walked through it and immediately came to a dead stop. He had heard curious scrambling, scratching sounds. Rats? What else could it be? And then he heard whispered voices that most assuredly did not come from rats.

"Why didn' you close th' door behind yerself, jackass?" whispered one voice.

"And who was it fergot to lock the other door behind theirselves, double jackass?" whispered a second.

"Well, what was you doin' anyways, wakin' us all up?" came the first voice again.

"Had ter go ter the terlit, if you got ter know," was the reply.

"Aw, shut up, both o' you," whispered a third voice, which then added warily, "Who's there? Who is it who jist come in?"

Robin stood paralyzed. He could not even have said his name for his life.

"Whoever it is ain't speakin' ter us," came yet another voice. "Whyn't you jist light yer candle up again, Piggy, an' let's us have a look."

A match was struck, and a candle flared up. And Robin found himself looking into some of the meanest faces and sharpest eyes he had ever been that close to in his life, lodged in the bodies of four assorted boys. If ever he had looked at ragged street boys, he was surely looking at them now. A whole nest of them!

Chapter VII

St. Somethin'

⚓

For several moments the boys did nothing but stand and stare, although the fear in their faces instantly vanished as soon as they saw the nature of the unknown threat in the dark.

Then the boy with the candle, the smallest of the lot, who had a twisted leg that made him list heavily to one side, turned a pale, skinny face to the boy next to him. "Whyn't you arsk him agin, Duck?"

The boy addressed as Duck blew off his forehead a spike of dirty yellow hair, one of several decorating the top of his head, and narrowed his heavy-lidded pale blue eyes at Robin. "All right, you, we're arskin' you perlitely this time. We ain't goin' ter arsk so perlitely next. Wot's yer name, an wot're you doin' here?"

"I . . . I . . . I came in by accident," quavered Robin, close to collapsing.

The weedy, redheaded boy with a map of freckles on his face, and ears that stuck out from his head like flapjacks, hitched up his pants with his elbows, all swagger and boldness now that they knew what they were dealing with. "Well, you can't stay. Right, Duck?" he said.

"Right, Spider," Duck replied through clenched teeth.

"I . . . I only wanted to stay the night where it's warm," said Robin faintly.

"An' hidin' wot you got in that bundle yer carryin', an' that bag." The fourth boy swiped the drizzle from his stubby nose with the back of his arm, and then looked at the others with raised eyebrows. "An' maybe leadin' somebody chasin''im right here ter us. Ain't that so?"

"Sounds so ter me, Mouse. You got a pernt." Duck glared at Robin. "Wot you got in that there bundle?"

"It's . . . it's my baby brother," Robin said. "And . . . and what's in the bag are his milk, and . . ."

"He's lyin'," Spider interrupted.

"Lyin'," agreed Mouse and Piggy.

"Show us wot you got," Duck said. He took a menacing step toward Robin. "C'mon, show us."

"Show us," the boys echoed, following Duck.

It was at that moment, just as they were advancing on Robin, that Danny chose to open his eyes, screw up his little face, and start bawling his head off.

Robin, bone weary, empty from having had practically nothing for supper, and now scared out of his wits, felt his legs crumple, as a black curtain came down over him.

When Robin came to a few minutes later, he was lying on the ground with his cap tossed off to one side, his jacket unbuttoned. His head, which was now hurting fiercely, was resting on a pile of rags. He could not at first remember where he was. All he could see by the light of a single fluttering candle was four boys sitting on the ground in a circle. One of them was holding a candle. It took him a few moments to remember who the boys were.

"Piggy, you ain't doin' it right," one of them was saying.

"Looky here, Spider," was the reply, "me ma had more babies 'n yers, an' I got stuck takin' care o' most o' the lot. You don't know spit 'bout it more'n I do."

Babies! Danny! Robin struggled to sit up as fast as his hurting head would allow. Where was Danny?

And then he saw his little brother—in the arms of the boy called Piggy, who was sitting surrounded by the other boys. Robin dimly remembered their names as being Mouse, Spider, and Duck. Piggy was holding a bottle, from which Danny was sucking for all his worth, looking contendedly up into Piggy's face.

"Look, all o' you," said Spider, the freckle-faced redhead, "the baby's brother done woke up."

"Don't worry none," said the spike-haired Duck. "We got yer brother took care o'. All o' us growed up 'round a ma wot had so many babies you couldn't o' swung a bleedin' cat an' not hit one."

"We even changed his dipe," said Mouse proudly, with a grin that not only wrinkled his stubby nose, but displayed an enormous gap between his two front teeth. "You c'n rinch it out in the sink down the hall. This church got a room down here wot's got a ter-lit wot actual cleans out when you go pullin' a chain. An' it got this sink in the hallway wot runs hot an' cold."

Spider pulled on an ear, and shook his head, frowning. "I d'no, Mouse. Don't seem right rinchin' a dipe in holy water."

Duck gave a disgusted sigh. "Wot you got inside o' that head o' yers, Spider, ants runnin' round? Wot's holy 'bout it? Same basin wot the old man probable uses ter rinch out his mops. Mops is used ter mop the floor. You think as how rich people's feet's any cleaner 'n' anyone else wot walks on the floor? They probable steps in dog poop like anyone else if they ain't lookin'. Ain't nobody said dog poop's holy wot I ever heard 'bout."

"Maybe," said Spider, demolished.

"No maybe 'bout it," said Duck, turning again to Robin. "Anyways, you c'n stay the night if it suits you," he said indifferently.

"Th-thank you," said Robin, faltering, for he was still having trouble taking in all that was happening.

"You ate anythin' recent?" Duck asked him.

Robin shook his head.

"Maybe that's why he folded," Mouse said. "We got that end

o' sausich an' some bread still. Anybody cares if I give it ter' 'im?"

Nobody appeared to care, so Mouse went over to the front wall, rummaged around in a cardboard box and carried back in his hands the sausage and a chunk of bread, both of which he thrust unceremoniously at Robin.

"Thank you very much," said Robin, hungrily taking a big bite of the sausage. Nothing had ever tasted so good to him, and it was, in truth, a very good quality of sausage. He wondered how the boys had come by it. Stolen, without doubt.

"Maybe he'd like some water," Spider said. "I'll take a cup an' go git 'im some."

"You mean some o' that holy water wot's been blessed by the pope?" said Duck, exchanging grins with Mouse.

"Aw, shut up!" said Spider, turning red to the tips of his ears. He lit a candle and went stumping from the room.

"Yeah, you had better shut up," Piggy said in a low voice. "The baby's eyes is gettin' heavy, an' he's goin' back ter sleep. Mouse, you come git 'im and lay 'im over on that nest o' rags in the corner out o' the light."

Mouse gently picked up Danny from Piggy's arms and laid him down on the rags. By then Spider was already coming through the door with the cup of water. Then the boys all dropped down around Robin, waiting until he had drained the cup.

"Cornsider yerself blessed," Duck said, casting another wicked grin in Mouse's direction. "An' now maybe you'd like ter tell us wot yer doin' here with that baby wot you say's yer brother."

Robin looked nervously from one boy to the next—street boys. He had seen how they teased one another. What would they have to say to his plan to leave Danny on the steps of the church in the hope that some wealthy family would take him home and care for him? How could they know, or care, how desperate he was to have come up with such a plan?

"We're waitin'," said Duck.

Robin gulped. He felt he had no choice but to make up some acceptable lie, but for his life he could think of none. He would just have to tell the truth.

"I . . . I . . . I was going to leave him on the church steps in the morning and . . . and . . . and . . ." Robin stopped, trying to find the courage to go on.

"You was goin' ter leave him on the steps," Piggy went on for him quite matter of factly, "figgerin' as how someone wot got lots o' money would see wot a nice baby he were, and take 'im home. Ain't that so?"

Robin nodded. "But . . . but I was going to find out who took him," he blurted. "Then I would go and beg them to let me see him sometimes. I couldn't . . . I couldn't bear it never to see him again."

"Nobody's goin' ter pick 'im up," said Mouse. "It don't even work when you take babies and leave 'em right on the doorstep o' rich people's houses. Me ma had thoughts o' it til she found out wot happens ter them babies wot gits left on doorsteps."

"Rich people got their own babies," Duck broke in. "They don't want none wot come from the tenements. Nex' mornin' after the baby gits left, he gits took ter the police station. It spends a cozy night there, then gits took ter a infants' hospital off on an islan' someplace. Don't last long there neither. Not 'cause it gits took someplace else, but 'cause it dies, makin' room fer the nex' one. So wot you goin' ter do next?"

What Robin was going to do next was throw his hands to his face to hide the tears that had flooded his eyes. Crying in front of street boys! Sure death! But his life was no longer worth much anyway. His only hope for saving Danny had just been snatched away from him. Running away had indeed been madness. There was nothing left for him but to return to Hawker Doak. Let these street boys tease and taunt him. What difference did it make now?

And then he felt a grimy, torn rag poked into his hands.

"Did yer ma send you ter do it?" Duck asked. His voice was perfectly flat, no hint of teasing or taunting in it.

Robin shook his head, rubbing his eyes with the rag. "She's dead," he mumbled into it.

"Wot 'bout yer pa?" asked Spider.

Robin looked up from the rag. "He died a year ago."

"So you been livin' by yerself with yer brother?" asked Piggy.

"No," replied Robin. "We were with my stepfather."

"Were he the one wot sent you ter leave yer brother on the church steps?" asked Duck.

Robin shook his head again. "It . . . it was my idea."

Piggy frowned. "An' he never done nothin' 'bout stoppin' you?"

"He never knew I was going to do it," said Robin. "He doesn't even know I've gone. I . . . I . . . I'm running away from him."

The boys all looked at one another. "Were he hittin' you?" Mouse asked.

Robin nodded. "But that wasn't why I was running away. It was because I saw he was going to hit my baby brother. I snatched him away, but what if I wasn't there next time? Next time he might be killed."

"An' he ain't got no ma ter pertect 'im neither," said Spider.

"So wot you goin' ter do?" Mouse asked.

Robin shrugged. "Go back to him, I guess. He's sending me to the factories. I'm eleven, but he's making me lie and say I'm fourteen. My brother gets put in a baby farm. I expect he'll die there if my stepfather doesn't kill him. It's . . . it's murder either way."

"You said as how yer step-pa hits you?" Duck asked. "Did he hit you hard?"

Robin nodded.

"If you got bruises ter prove it, why not you show us?" said Duck.

"Why'd you want 'im ter do that, Duck?" Spider asked.

"Prove he's not lyin'," said Duck.

"Wot do we care?" Mouse said. "He's only stayin' the night."

"I'd jist like ter know," Duck said. He gave Robin a narrow-eyed look. "C'mon, show us!"

Robin agreed with Mouse. What difference did it make if he had bruises or not? But Duck appeared to be the ringleader of this batch of street boys, and could send Robin back out into the chilling night with Danny, to make his way back to Hawker Doak. Robin threw off his jacket and dropped it on the floor. Then he started to peel off his shirt.

"All right!" Duck said quickly. "You don't got ter go no further. If yer willin' ter show 'em, then you must got 'em. But now I'm arskin' you ter take yerself out inter the hallway and close the door behin' you. I got ter have a meetin' with me friends here."

"The friends" looked as puzzled as Robin felt as he trailed into the hallway and closed the door. But he was ready to do anything asked of him as long as he could stay the rest of the night, and Danny was not in danger. And who knew but what in the morning with his mind clearer, he might have some new idea as to where he and Danny could go that was not back to Hawker.

But the longer Robin stood outside the door in the dark hall, the more he began to think about a new worry. Street boys were pickpockets and thieves, were they not? And there was his jacket lying on the floor in that room without its owner inside it. The two dollars and fifty cents could disappear. The pin and locked could disappear, so if he had to go back to Hawker, they could not be secretly returned to the drawer. And the treasured nickel watch that belonged to his papa could also disappear. It seemed an eternity before the door opened and he was invited back into the candlelit room.

Piggy, Mouse, and Spider were staring at him with curious half grins on their faces. Duck, on the other hand, looked deadly serious.

"Seen yer eyes flippin' over ter yer jacket," he said. "But you don't got ter worry none. Wotever you got in it ain't been touched. We don't steal no more, an' we especial don't steal from someone wot's one o' us. An' we believes now as how yer that. We never knowed fer certain. You talk better'n us, an' you ain't near so raggy lookin'. It's why I had to arsk you 'bout them bruises. Wanted ter prove you wasn't lyin' 'bout nothin'. An' we all b'lieves as you wasn't. So, at our meetin' I arsked everyone ter put up a hand if they wanted ter arsk you ter join up with us, an' everyone put up their hand. So now I'm arskin' you."

Robin's knees felt weak. Most of his life he had dreaded and feared street boys. Now, just when he so desperately needed to find a home for himself and Danny, it was street boys who were offering him one.

"But . . . but what about my baby brother?" he stammered faintly.

"All been figgered out," said Piggy, now producing a full-fledged, ear-to-ear grin. "Ought we ter tell him now, Duck?"

"Aw, it's gittin' late," Duck said. "We better wait 'til mornin'. But he ain't yet said if he's joinin' up with us. So, is you, or ain't you?" he asked Robin.

Robin did not wait to draw another breath. "I am," he said simply.

"But you ain't even telled yer name," Mouse said. "You got a name, aint' you?"

Robin hesitated. Should he lie and invent something? After all, remember what Hawker's friend Maggot had said, how he had better start calling himself something else just for protection? But then Robin thought of what his papa always used to say. "In for a penny, in for a pound." So go ahead and give his real name. Let the boys laugh and get it over wth.

"It's Robin," he said, as defiantly as he dared.

Nobody even snickered.

"It's the name o' some kind o' bird, ain't it?" said Piggy.

"It's nice," mused Spider. "We all got a kind o' animal name, an' now we got 'nother one."

"Spider ain't a animal," said Piggy.

"Closer'n some," said Spider. "But wot 'bout the baby. Wot's 'is name?"

"It's not any kind of animal," replied Robin. "It's just Danny."

"Don't matter none," said Mouse. "We'll jist pertend there's a bird wot got the name o' Danny."

"Danny the bird wot come ter live with us at St. Somethin'," said Piggy, yawning hugely, for the hour was late indeed.

The yawn was contagious, and the rest all followed suit.

"But . . . but what's St. Something?" asked Robin.

Duck looked at him sleepily and yawned again. "It's where yer at, Robin. Wot did you think? Yer bed's anywheres on the floor where there ain't somebody else. You already got your pillow."

Duck collapsed on the floor where the other boys were already curled up on their rag pillows, and reached over to snuff out the candle.

"G'night!" he said.

"G'night!" chorused Piggy, Spider, and Mouse.

Conversation for the night was clearly over. If Robin was to learn anything more, it was going to have to wait until morning. But everything had happened so suddenly, and then ended so abruptly, his head was still spinning when he lay down. In one day he had become a thief, liar, and runaway. But most unbelievably of all, in less than a heartbeat it seemed, he had become a street boy. And he had the feeling there would be a great deal more to learn about *that*. Oh yes, a great deal more indeed!

Chapter VIII

Duck's Tale

⁂

Nobody was very cheerful about Danny waking them up in the morning, soaking wet and screaming for his breakfast. The only one who did not appear to mind as much as the others was Piggy. He quickly retrieved a clean diaper and the remaining bottle of milk from Robin's shopping bag, and scuttled over as fast as his twisted leg could carry him to relieve Danny's misery.

Robin, having spent his first night with nothing between himself and a rock-hard floor, and with recent events whirling in his brain, had managed to get little sleep. In truth, he had only fallen asleep a short time before Danny issued his loud demand for attention. He only manged to stumble over to him as Piggy was already removing his sodden diaper.

"I'll take it over, Piggy," he said uncomfortably. "You don't need to do it."

"I don't mind none. You'll git yer chance. You c'n tend ter this, an' one here from las' night, an' the dirty bottle," Piggy said, waving the wet diapers at Robin. "You c'n rinch 'em out when you goes ter the terlit. Looks like the rest o' the boys is now goin', so they'll show you where it's at. You c'n take over when you git back, an' I'll git my terlit turn."

So Robin joined the three other boys, all yawning and rubbing their eyes, in a parade led by Mouse, who was holding the fluttering candle. A candle was, of course, needed, for the hallway was as dark in the daytime as it had been at night. The parade ended at what Mouse informed Robin was "the room wot had the terlit." After they had all had their turns at this particular accomodation, the other two returned to their rooms, while Mouse held the candle for Robin to take care of Danny's laundry with a cake of soap found at the sink. As he scrubbed, Mouse continued with his guided tour.

"Where the ol' geezer wot takes care o' down here an', we supposes, some o' the cleanin' upstairs, keeps 'is mops an' buckets," said Mouse, jerking his head at the other door farther down the hallway. "He got a small gas burner an' a ol' kettle wot he owns ter make tea for hisself. People here got ter be richer'n sin, puttin' all this stuff in wot's no more'n the bleedin' cellar. Better'n nothin' any o' us ever knowed."

"Aren't you afraid he'll discover you living down here?" asked Robin, squeezing the water from the diapers.

"Ain't yet. Course we ain't been here but a couple o' days," replied Mouse, as they started back down the hallway. "But we ain't worried none. He's deafer'n a door post. Got only one eye wot works, an' 'pears as how that ain't none too good. We knowed that 'fore we moved in when Duck seed him talkin' ter someone outside."

Just what Duck had seen, Robin would have to wait to hear, because they had now arrived back at their room, where Piggy was waiting to hand Danny over to him.

"You c'n hang the dipes over there on them chair legs," said Piggy, pointing to four chairs, each with only three remaining legs and holes punched in their cane seats, all turned upside down in a corner of the room. A pile of rags lay under the chairs.

Morning light now coming through the small window high in the wall also fell on the cardboard box that had held the sausage and bread, three wood boxes no more than a foot tall with brushes and rags stuffed in them, four mismatched cups, with broken handles, four mismatched, chipped plates, and a saucepan, a blackened, impossibly dented affair that could only have been salvaged from some city dump. But these items, all lined up neatly against the wall, gave every evidence that the boys had set up housekeeping there in earnest.

What very nearly brought tears to Robin's eyes, however, was the sight of the tiny tin spoon and bowl, and four empty baby bottles lined up along with the rest. This was as good as any other promise the boys could have made, that Danny was here to stay. And so, for that matter, was his big brother!

"Wot we got ter eat, Mouse?" Duck asked. "Got any o' that sausich left?"

"Aw, don't go eatin' when I ain't back yet," complained Piggy. "You all seed I were feedin' Danny an' ain't been ter the terlit. 'Sides, nobody as wot I c'n see took the saucepot ter git the drinkin' water."

"Git goin' and stop mewlin' 'bout it, Piggy. We ain't even set the table yet. We'll wait fer you an' the holy water," Duck said with a grin. It did look as if *that* joke was not going to die in a hurry.

Mouse, in the meantime, was rummaging around inside the cardboard box. "Yeah, we got 'nother lump o' sausich," he said. "Got some bread. Got a couple o' apples left."

"Them with all the worm holes?" asked Spider, wrinkling his nose.

"We an't never had no other kind, jackass," replied Mouse proudly. "You c'n spit out the worms like we always done."

This kind of conversation continued for a round or two before they were all seated on the floor in a circle, including the by-now-returned Piggy. Danny was already asleep peacefully on his rag cot. In front of the boys were the ragged assortment of cups and saucers, and in the center of the "table," set on a scrap of brown paper, were the sausage, bread, apples, and a bent knife about as black as the saucepan.

"I'll share a cup an' plate with Robin," Spider said, as Duck cut chunks of sausage with the unwieldy knife, and passed them around.

"Don't 'spect good eats like this here every time," Duck said as he handed Robin his chunk of sausage. "This here's bought special 'cause we was havin' a party 'bout movin' here. Never ate nothin' like sausich when we was livin' under the pier. Had mostly bread. Taters when we was lucky. If we c'd git a fire goin', we cooked 'em in the saucepot."

"Jist like we c'n cook 'em here on the gas burner," said Spider. "We c'n cook here jist 'bout any ol' time, an' jist 'bout any ol' thing we want. Even make usselves a cup o' tea when we git a rainy day," he ended dreamily.

"We can't cook nothin' like cabbages," said Mouse, bringing Spider back down to earth. "Somebody'll be lookin' in every room ter see wot might o' died if we done anythin' jackassy stoopid like that."

"No use talkin' 'bout wot we're goin' ter eat and wot we're not goin' ter eat if they ain't nothin' ter eat, which right now they ain't," Duck said. "Not even no bread. One o' us is got ter go git somethin' after we're done workin'."

Go get something, Robin thought. Milk! There was not only no food left for all the boys, there was nothing for Danny either, and he would have to have his milk by the middle of the morning. There could be no waiting until after work, whatever that work was.

"I'll go," Robin said quickly. "I'll take Danny with me and go. I can carry things in my shopping bag. But . . . but he has to have milk this morning."

"If you want ter do that," Duck said. "Wot we c'n do is all put in maybe three cents, an' you c'n get wot yer able fer that."

"Oh, you don't need to put in anything," Robin said at once. "I'll pay for it all. I . . . I'd like to."

"You got the money?" Duck's eyebrows went sailing up his

forehead. "Where'd you git it? We ain't got 'round ter askin' wot you do fer work, but wotever it was, didn't yer step-pa take it all 'way from you?"

"I never worked," said Robin, feeling his face redden. "I . . . I just went to school and then helped my mama with Danny. She hid some money in the kitchen, and told me about it before she died. That's what I have now."

"How much you got?" asked Mouse.

What, tell street boys how much money he had in his pocket? What kind of madness would that be? Yet had they not already had the opportunity to take everything he had, including his watch? And were they not trusting him with their hard-earned money to go shopping? But more than anything, there were the baby bottles and the tiny tin spoon and bowl lined up against the wall with probably all the boys had in the world. What, tell these street boys how much money he had in his pocket? Yes, of course! Why would he not do it?

"I . . . I have two dollars and fifty cents," he said.

Two dollars and fifty cents? A fortune by the sound of the collective whistles around the breakfast table.

But Piggy then frowned and shook his head. "Sounds like a heap, but you can't be spendin' it on us. You got ter save it fer Danny. Milk don't come cheap. Right?"

"Right!" they all agreed.

"An'," said Duck, "'pears as how you ain't earnin' nothin' neither. You jist been goin' ter school. You was goin' ter leave yer baby brother on the steps o' this here church, but how was you goin' ter take care o' yerself after the two dollars an' fifty cents were gone?"

Robin threw out his hands helplessly. "Sell papers, I guess."

"Which you never done b'fore," said Duck. "In yer guessin', was you guessin' as how you got ter buy yer first stack o' papers 'fore you c'n go sellin'?"

"N-n-no," stammered Robin.

"Takes some o' yer money right there," offered Spider.

"An' then findin' a good corner wot ain't been took by some other bleedin' paper boy," said Duck. "An' then if he finds you there tryin' ter horn in on his biz, you might jist's well kiss off the rest o' yer bleedin' life."

"Then," said Mouse, "night comes, an' you still got most o' yer stack left. Nex' day you got ter buy 'nother stack, only you never made no money the day b'fore ter buy it. So back you goes ter yer two dollars an' fifty cents, which now ain't two dollars an' fifty cents no more. Then the nex' day . . ."

"Aw, can it, Mouse," said Duck. "He's got the picter by now."

He did indeed get the "picter." And was feeling more and more beaten down by it. What had ever made him think he could survive on the streets? And before he came up with the idea of the church steps, which of course had gone the way of all his other ideas, what had made him think he could take care of himself *and* Danny? It appeared that he could not have even taken care of himself very well. And now it had gone back to being himself *and* Danny. The "picter" was no longer merely bleak, it was totally hopeless!

"It doesn't matter any more that I don't know the first thing about selling papers," he said. "How can I go out and do anything and leave Danny? Who would take care of him? You heard what Mouse said. Milk doesn't come cheap. My money would soon go, and then what?"

Robin saw nothing funny in what he had just said, yet why were all the boys suddenly grinning at one another? Happy to have a reason to kick him out, were they? Did not perhaps like being awakened in the morning by Danny howling? Realized they had made a big mistake taking the two of them in, had they?

"Well, so happens the 'wot' is already been figgered out," said Duck, his grin broadening. "We got it all figgered out b'fore we even arsked you ter join up. Piggy's who's goin' ter take care o' yer Danny."

"P–P–Piggy?" said Robin. "H–h–how?"

"Tell 'im, Piggy," said Duck.

"*You* tell 'im," returned Piggy.

"Ain't it time somebody telled 'im somethin' 'bout *all* o' us?" Mouse said. "Robin's done telled us 'bout hisself, but none o' us is said nothin' 'bout where we come from nor how we come here. Ain't it proper we ought ter do that? Then he'll know 'bout Piggy an' the rest o' us. Duck, whyn't you do it?"

"Well," said Duck, "all o' us met whilst we was paper boys. It's why we knows so much 'bout it. We was friends wot found out we all got a ma what had more kids'n you c'n count. We all had a pa wot beat us regular when we brung home less'n wot he were expectin' from sellin' papers. You got ter know it ain't jist a step–pa wot beats his kids. An' we got beat a lot more when our pa come in from visitin' at the corner."

"Anyways, Piggy's pa decided as how Piggy weren't makin' 'nough with the papers. Like yer step–pa, he figgered as how he'd put Piggy in the fac'tries. Piggy don't look nowhere near sixteen, so his pa tol' the boss at the fact'ry Piggy c'd read an' write ter get by passin' fer fourteen. Piggy ain't able ter pass fer ten, but them fact'ry bosses never even arsk you ter prove yer readin' an writin' if they wants you bad 'nough. They wanted Piggy, 'cause he used ter be like a monkey way he got 'round. Then he felled inter this m'chinery which ruint his leg. Fact'ry didn't want him no more, but his pa thinks it ain't so bad, 'cause he's still good fer goin' beggin' on the streets. Only jist like when he was sellin' papers, if he never brought in wot his pa thought he ought ter, he got beat jist like b'fore. His pa'd say he weren't beggin' good 'nough."

This was turning into a long story, and Duck had to stop to take a deep breath before going on. "Well, seein' poor Piggy got us all thinkin' as how we'd had 'nough o' the beatin's, so we runned off an' joined up with boys wot live under the pier near the big fish fact'ry down by the river. Went on sellin' papers, but

never took none o' it home no more. All o' us but Piggy was savin'
ter git boxes, an' brushes, an' blackin' ter go inter the biz o' shoe
shinin'. Piggy had ter go on beggin' 'cause he ain't able ter do
much else yet."

"Didn't anybody's mama or papa go looking for them?" asked
Robin, knowing how distraught his own would have been had he
just disappeared into thin air like that.

All four boys shrugged. "Maybe they did, or maybe they never
did. We never arsked," Spider said. "All we knowed were nobody
come lookin' fer us, which never surprised us none. We heard
'bout a boy we knowed wot sold papers an' got drownded. When
he got found, we was telled, nobody knowed as how he'd even
been missin'. With so many in the family, one more nor less don't
mean nothin'. So go on with yer story, Duck."

"Well," Duck said, "knowin' as how we was all goin' ter have
ter find places ter set up our biz, an' how streets wot looked
richer'n others might be jist the right places, I come up on this
here church. It were gettin' on dark, but outside I seed this pretty
lady talkin' ter a ol' man wot she were havin' ter shout at 'cause he
were hard o' hearin'. He had a eye patch an' kep' puttin' his head
for'ard like a old rooster, which said as how he couldn't see too
good neither. the lady was comin' from the church an' was carryin'
some flowers wot had their heads droopin'. I follered the ol' man
ter the back o' the church, thinkin' as how I'd bring them flowers
back ter the pier.

"The ol' man put the flowers on the steps, then like ter o'
broke his neck climbin' down 'em. I waited an' I waited. Then he
comes back, an' if he don't go an' pick up them flowers, keepin'
them fer hisself. But wot I seed was he fergitted an' lef' the key in
the door. So I jist let meself in, an' lighted me candle. Liked wot I
seed. Couldn't b'lieve my eyes, but seed a bunch o' keys hangin'
on the wall, an' one were jist like the big one in the door. Then
I figgered as how a ol' man wot fergits a key in a lock, likely's

fergitted one he had hangin' on the wall. So I helps myself ter it. An' here we is."

"You telled it good, Duck," Mouse said. "But you never telled wot you telled us 'bout the Landlord."

"Landlord?" asked Robin, landlords as of that very morning being greatly on his mind.

"Tell it!" said Spider and Piggy.

"Aw," said Duck, "it's jist when I thought as how I'd like fer us ter be movin' in here, I ought ter be askin' a landlord. Then it come ter me as how the Landlord o' this here place'd be Him wot were 'bove me. Telled Him how good we'd be if He made it so's we c'd come live here. Which says why were sittin' roun' a table proper 'stead o' jist sittin' any ol' place an' shovin' in the food like we all done when we was livin' under the pier."

"We all aim ter be havin' a warsh at the sink too," said Mouse. "Outside it ain't noticed much, but inside we probable smell bad as cabbage cookin'."

"Anyways," said Duck. "Maybe it's why we never got a mind ter turn you out when you showed up. It . . . it ain't wot the Landlord would o' done."

"Aw, c'mon, Duck, you know as how we wanted ter do it," said Piggy. "We wouldn't o' turned 'im out with Danny anyways. But now it looks like we got way off from wot we was talkin' 'bout, an' that's how it's me wot's goin' ter take care o' Danny whilst you goes out, Robin."

"Are you certain, Piggy?" Robin asked.

"I ain't never wanted ter go back beggin'," Piggy said. "Now I don't got ter do it. My job's takin' care o' yer Danny. Yers is earnin'."

"But what can I do?" asked Robin. "None of you think I'd be much good at selling newspapers. Could . . . could I do shoe shining?"

"Don't see why not," said Duck. "It ain't so easy's sellin' papers, but ain't so dangerous neither. You c'n take a bit o' yer money ter buy yer box an' brushes. An' oncet you git 'em, you don't never need ter git 'em agin."

"How will I learn what to do?" asked Robin.

"Come roun' with one o' us," said Mouse. "We'll see you learn good an' proper."

Piggy grinned. "You'll be the pa goin' out ter make money. I'll be the ma stayin' home ter look after the baby. Ain't that somethin'?"

"It's somethin', all right," said Duck. "But we got ter git goin', an' you got ter be gittin' out fer Danny's milk, Robin. The ol' man'll probable be here when you git back, an' have the lamp on in the hallway, so sneak in real careful."

"I will," said Robin. "And you might as well know I *am* going to get the other food. I'll be making all the money back in a hurry. You'll see." Then he added proudly, "I'm going to be a shoe-shine boy with the rest of you now!"

"The Serciety o' Shoe-shine Boys o' St. Somethin'," said Spider. "Now that's somethin' else, ain't it?"

"Is that really the name of this church?" Robin asked. "St. Something?"

"Nah!" said Duck. "We don't know wot it is, none o' us bein' able ter read the sign wot's in front. But most o' the churches wot we know 'bout's called St. Somethin' or other. So we jist calls this one St. Somethin'."

St. Something! Well, it could have been St. Anything for all Robin cared. What difference did the name make? He had found a home for himself and Danny. He had found friends. He was even going into business for himself as a member of the Society of Shoe-shine Boys of St. Something. And Hawker Doak's "scrawny little weasel" had done this all in the space of only a few hours. It was, as Spider would have said, "somethin' else"!

Chapter IX

A Disappointing Discovery

᛭

That night, courtesy of a trip by Spider to a dump, a fifth place setting appeared on their "table." The plate was, if possible, more chipped than the others, and the cup was missing a handle entirely. But who was there who noted these things? Certainly not Robin. For courtesy of himself, the boys were enjoying the feast of their lives!

There was more sausage, with some to spare, and bread actually bought fresh rather than from the stall of the stale-bread lady. There was a grand wedge of cheese, some sweet biscuits, and an apple each, with hardly enough worm holes to raise a single eyebrow. There was even a pound of tea leaves, for tea to be made on the gas burner down the hall, served with a liberal pouring of sugar from a paper sack, and then stirred with the only utensil available, the black, bent knife. And, of course, there was fresh milk for Danny.

Emboldened by his successful shopping venture, and by making it safely back ito their cellar room, Robin had actually gone back out again and returned with a box, brushes, and blacking, ready for his first lessons in shoe shining. This latter, unfortunately, what with his extravagant spending on food, had dangerously depleted his money supply.

"You shouldn't o' ought ter done all this," Duck said, with a worried frown.

Robin knew full well he "shouldn't o' ought ter." He had less than a dollar left! Still, he was not going to spoil everybody's good time by remarking on this. And after all, he was sure that he would make the money back in a hurry. Right now, he would try to overlook the queasy feeling he had in the pit of his stomach that he might have been dipping into Danny's milk money.

When the enormously successful supper ended, the boys lounged about sipping their cups of sweet tea, and discussing the events of the day. Business had not been very good for any of them. But what with their full stomachs and the warming effect of cups of well-sugared tea, nobody seemed much bothered by it. Tomorrow was another day, an opportunity to do better.

Piggy then had the grand idea that Danny ought to be started on his "porritch" along with his milk. So Robin went down the hall to prepare a bit from the sack of cereal he had brought with him. Of course, he had to use the same battered black saucepot in which tea had been brewed. He vowed to himself that one day, after he had made all that money he was preparing to make, he was going to buy the boys a brand new shining saucepot.

At any rate, another entertaining event was added to the evening as they all sat with eyes glued to Piggy holding Danny while Robin fed him with his tiny tin spoon. More of the "porritch" ended up outside Danny than inside him, but everyone generally approved the performance.

"Keep him sleepin' later," said Mouse, certainly a good thing to remember considering the hollering that had greeted them early that morning.

The next suggestion, one made by Robin, was not so successful. He asked if he could have a shoe-shine lesson, now he was all ready with his box and brushes.

"On wot?" asked Duck. "Ain't you never took a good look at wot we got on our feet? Yer own shoes ain't too great, but nex' ter ours, yers might o' comed off'n a store shelf."

There was no arguing with what Duck had said. Robin's shoes were such that all the blacking and polishing in the world could have done little to improve them, but at least they covered all of his feet. The boys' shoes were no better than the torn rags they wore on their backs. Besides being layered with filth from the streets, the shoes had soles so separated from the tops they flapped as the boys walked. Their bare toes poked from holes cut out in front, for the shoes had long since been outgrown, and dirty pieces of string served as shoelaces.

Anything Robin might have wanted to say lay stuck in his throat.

"No need ter say nothin'," said Duck. "But how you'll get teached is by hangin' roun' one o' us all day an' watchin'. Tomorrow you come with me. Nex' day maybe Mouse. Nex' maybe Spider. You c'n try a hand with proper shoes. Never you mind. *You'll* learn."

"Duck," Mouse said, "if Robin's goin' out in the streets, shouldn' we ought ter tell 'im 'bout our danger sign?"

"Yer right, Mouse," Duck replied. "He ought ter know it. Robin, it's jist that if yer ever in trouble, an' one o' us is near 'nough ter see it, you jist hold a hand by yer side an' curl up yer fingers inter a fist. That's if it ain't safe ter holler at us. None o' us is ever had a need o' usin' it, but you never know. You jist never know. Now, let's see you doin' it."

"Hey, I got a idea," said Mouse, after they had all approved Robin's efforts at making a fist. "Wot 'bout dice? We ain't played 'em since we done left the pier."

"Nah," said Duck. "We ain't goin' ter do that no more. Promised the Landlord. No stealin'. No cheatin'. No gamblin'."

"Aw, sounds like no nothin'," grumbled Mouse. "Wot a life!" But he must have agreed with Duck, because there was "no arguin'" either!

"I got a idea," said Spider. "How's 'bout we have a worsh? We said we was goin' ter."

"That's some bleedin' idea, Spider," said Mouse. "Yuck!"

"Ain't nothin' wrong with it," said Duck. "Spider's right. It's wot we said. But no need ter do all top an' bottom o' us at one time. Ternight we c'n do tops. Bottoms nex' time. I'll go first ter show you I ain't goin' ter get kilt doin' it."

Yanking off his shirt, he dropped it on the floor and snatched up a rag from under the chairs where Danny's drying diapers were draped. Then he lit a candle and disappeared out the door. They could hear his shoes determinedly flap, flap, flapping down the hallway. A short while later, they flap, flap, flapped back again. Their owner, for lack of a towel, was dripping wet from the top of his head to the rope that held up his pants. After shaking his head like a dog just come in from a swim in a pond, he threw his shirt back on over his wet body.

"Brrr!" he said, shivering but still managing to look very pleased with himself. "Must o' shed a pound o' dirt. Yer turn, Spider."

After that, Spider, Mouse, and Piggy made their trips down the hallway, returning looking just as pleased and proud of themselves as Duck had over the achievement. Robin went as well, choosing not to mention that he had had a good wash at his own kitchen sink a day earlier.

He really did want to be one of them, for he had come to have a very different idea about street boys. They had a code of honor. For all the rude names they called each other, and the teasing, they were loyal friends who stuck together and supported each other. And now he had even learned something else. Under their shirts they had the same chicken-skinny bodies as he did. Oh yes, Robin now had a very different idea about street boys.

At the moment, however, for four of them the only thing on their minds was the curious feeling of being clean. Well, half clean, anyway.

"Problem with havin' a worsh," said Duck, "is it makes wot we got on feel dirtier'n b'fore."

"An' all tore up," said Spider. "Wish we knowed somethin' bout' sewin'.'"

"Sewin'!" said Mouse. "You really do got butterflies in yer head, Spider."

Robin took a moment to consider this situation. Well, in for a penny, in for a pound. "I . . . I can sew," he said. "I . . . I used to help my mama, I mean my ma, with sewing she took in when we needed money."

Duck's eyes widened. "You mean you c'd sew some o' these rags up fer us?"

"If I had a needle and some thread," replied Robin.

Duck just shook his head and grinned. "Well I'll be!" he said. "Sewin'! So I were right. I figgered as you *got* ter be good fer *somethin'!*"

Only one thing marred what had been an otherwise happy day for Robin. When Piggy had managed to sneak from the room to make a visit down the hallway, Robin had quickly pulled from his jacket the locket he had had no chance to look at from the time he had taken it from Hawker's drawer. He snapped the locket open. And there were indeed pictures in it, one of a beautiful young woman, and one of a handsome young man. But they were not of his mama and papa. It was a bitter disappointment.

He hid the locket back inside his jacket where it would have to remain with the pin. After all, he could never show either locket or pin to the boys. "No stealin', no cheatin', no gamblin'," Duck had said. Robin did not want to start his life with them as a known thief. Oh, how he wished he had never heard of Hawker Doak's precious drawer!

Chapter X

A Startling Scene

𝕋 *alking* about being a shoe-shine boy turned out to be a lot easier than *being* one, Robin soon learned. It was, in truth, downright frightening, even though all he was doing was standing beside Duck and watching him do the work. Robin had not even brought his own box and brushes with him, as he certainly never expected to do any shoe shining that day.

What he found out was that not everyone simply came up to a shoe-shine boy and said, "Shine, please." No, not at all. More often than not, the boy had to go up to a likely prospect, get his attention, and say, "Shine your shoes, mister?"

And though selling newspapers may have been a difficult business, at least all a boy did when he sold a paper was hand it over and take the money. If the paper had bad news in it, that was not the boy's fault. It was the fault of the paper, and that was that. The newspaper boy was not blamed if the news was not to the customer's liking.

The shoe-shine boy, on the other hand, was selling his services, and they had to be right or he would hear about it, and possibily not even be paid. Further, the services had to be performed under the very eyes of the owner of the shoes, eyes making certain that every penny's worth of value was received, and no mistakes made. Robin had his first sad lesson in mistake making that very day.

Unsuspecting, he watched Duck persuade a man to have his shoes shined, only to have a brush thrust into his hands as Duck said under his breath, "Here! Yer ready ter have a go at it."

Robin, of course, was no such thing, and soon proved it by trembling so hard he got blacking on the man's trouser cuff. The man swore at him and walked off in a rage, saying he ought to charge him for a new pair of trousers. Quite naturally, neither Duck nor Robin earned any money for this job.

"Sorry fer that," said Duck. "Guess you wasn't ready like I thought. Never you mind. I messed up the firs' time I ever done shoes. You'll git it soon."

"I'll pay you back for this one," said Robin, totally miserable.

"Nah, fergit it," said Duck. "Whyn't you go on back. I'll be followin' soon. You had 'nough lessons fer terday. An' ain't goin' ter be long fer it ter be gittin' dark."

Robin, feeling as if he had had all the lessons he ever wanted in the art of shoe shining, trailed dejectedly back to the church. It would be the greatest miracle the church had ever witnessed if he ever learned to shine a pair of shoes. The only problem was, what else was there that he could do? The worry occupied his mind all the way, and was only driven out, when he arrived at the church, by what for a while seemed an even greater worry.

The old man always left the cellar door unlocked during the day. The door had to be opened very carefully, however, because he might be close behind it at any time. So Robin slowly inched the door open. The old man was nowhere to be seen in the hallway, but something was wrong. Light was coming through the doorway of their room! Worse than that, so were voices!

One of the other boys must have returned and was talking to Piggy. But why were they being so careless as to leave the door open? They all knew they could lose their home in the church cellar if they were found out. Or had they already been found out? Were the voices coming from the room those of Piggy—and the old man? Robin crept closer to the doorway. The terrors of learning to shine shoes were now replaced by something far worse. For if they had been found out, where would he and Danny go? Follow the boys back to the pier? Return to Hawker Doak? Slowly, slowly, Robin crept closer to the open doorway, until he was able to peek in. And there he saw the old man in there with Piggy—and Danny!

But beyond finding the old man, what a startling scene it was that greeted Robin's eyes! For Piggy was seated cross-legged on the floor. Across from him the old man sat on an upturned bucket. Both were sipping a drink from the chipped, broken-handled cups. And between them, lying on a faded blue blanket, full of holes but otherwise spotlessly clean, lay Danny. He was on his back, gurgling happily as he waved his little arms in the air, reaching for a bit of red rag the old man was dangling over him with his free hand.

"There we are! There's my little man!" he was saying as Robin, his jaw hanging open, came walking in.

"We got found out!" said Piggy happily, seeing Robin. "This here's Mr. Gribbins."

"Mr. Gribbins," said he, "wot ain't as deef as not ter be hearin' cryin' in his cellar, nor not so dim-witted's not ter know it come from a babby. An' even wiv my one eye, I ain't so blind's not ter know a babby when I sees one. Wot d'you think o' that?"

"This here's Robin," said Piggy.

"All right then," said Mr. Gribbins. "Wot d'you think o' that, Master Robin?"

Robin, needless to say, was so stunned he could hardly think at all. It was all he could to remember to close his jaw.

"Are . . . are . . . are you going to make us leave, Mr. Gribbins?" he was able to ask at last, his voice shaking.

"Wot?" exclaimed the old man. "And take this here sweet babby with you? You'll stay, but not jist 'cause o' the babby. I like the comp'ny, and I allus said as how there's all this room down here jist goin' ter waste. B'sides, I were in the streets when I were a lad. Sometimes someone were kind ter me. I'm jist passin' it on, you see. But mind, like I been tellin' yer Piggy, there's rules wot got to be follered. It's mostly jist this cellar wot's mine ter take care o', but I ain't goin' ter let no one go messin' with wot's upstairs neither."

"I told Mr. Gribbins 'bout wot we promised the Landlord," Piggy broke in. "No stealin', no cheatin', no gamblin'."

"It's the 'no stealin'' bit wot I got ter be consarned wiv," said Mr. Gribbins. "You ain't been upstairs, so you don't know wot I'm talkin' 'bout."

"Oh, we been upstairs. Went prowlin' the' first night we was here," said Piggy. "An' we never took nothin'."

"Wot 'bout the box up front wiv the hole up top?" asked Mr. Gribbins.

"Oh, we figgered as how them kind o' boxes is wot's put there ter collect fer the poor," Piggy said earnestly. "Even if we never maked a promise ter the Landlord, we'd never touch wot's meant fer the poor."

Mr. Gribbins took a long, hard look at Piggy with his one eye. "I think I got ter b'lieve you, Master Piggy," he said. "But I got ter git goin'. Hannah . . . her who is Missus Gribbins . . . she's ailin' an' can't go noplace. So she sits front o' the window watchin' fer me ter come home. When's the rest o' yer friends comin'?"

Mr. Gribbins had no sooner finished speaking than Mouse appeared with his shoe-shine box, standing slack-jawed at the doorway just as Robin had done. It was a minor church miracle that he was actually able to hang on to his box without letting it go crashing to the floor, for his face had gone as white as his shoe blacking was black.

"Mr. Gribbins, this here's Mouse. Mouse, this here's Mr. Gribbins," said Piggy who, without doubt noting Mouse's condition, hastened to add, "An' he says we c'n stay."

"Mr. Gribbins, wot ain't so deaf as not ter be hearin' cryin' in his cellar," he said, then repeating exactly all that had been said to Robin. He was clearly taking the greatest delight in making this speech. In truth, he repeated the same words for Duck and Spider when they finally appeared. That they all repeated the promises made to the Landlord, each without knowing what the others had said, gave him even more pleasure.

"Yer all good lads," he said as he was leaving. Then his one eye crinkled up as he smiled broadly. "Wait 'til Hannah hears 'bout the babby helpin' keep me comp'ny. She ain't goin' ter b'lieve it!" There was little doubt that Mr. Gribbins went home as happy a man as could be found in the city that night.

As for the boys, they could not stop talking about their good luck. Imagine it! Actually being allowed to live down there without having to sneak in and out and worry about being caught. Well, there was still *some* worry. For Mr. Gribbins had warned them that permission to live there should by all rights come from someone higher up the ladder than he was, he being at the very bottom.

"But it probable wouldn' be 'lowed," he had said. "Don't seem right. Rats move in without no permission from no one. But boys an' a babby ain't 'lowed. Ain't right's all I c'n say."

So care still had to be taken, but life would be easier than before. They could not believe their good luck, and talked about it all through their supper of the bits and pieces left over from the night before.

Duck had brought home with him a packet of needles and a spool of thread. Robin's promise to sew up their ragged clothes had not been forgotten. And as Duck was the one who had provided the needles and thread, it was fair that his shirt should be the first one repaired.

"I'll sew for an hour," Robin said, as Duck was peeling off his shirt. "I'd like to play with Danny a while before he goes to sleep."

"How'd you know wot's a hour?" asked Spider.

In for a penny, in for a pound! "I . . . I have a watch," Robin said, and went to pull it from his jacket.

"Is it a watch wot runs?" asked Mouse.

Robin nodded.

"You c'n tell time actual?" asked Piggy.

Robin nodded again.

"C'n we have a look?" Duck asked.

"Where'd you git it?" asked Mouse.

"It belonged to my papa," replied Robin. "But . . . but it's not real nickel or anything like that. It's . . . it's only plate." He could not, of course, forget what Mr. Slyke had said.

"Don't care if it's a cup an' saucer," Duck said. "None o' us ever had no watch. Never hope ter have one nice as this."

"Wot's the use o' one, Duck," said Mouse. "None o' us is able ter tell wot it says."

"Would you like to learn?" Robin asked. And from the looks on their faces, there was hardly any need for an answer.

So the evening ended up with the boys poring over his watch, arguing over what the big hand said and what the small hand did not say, as instructed by Robin. And Robin sat sewing on Duck's shirt with Danny by his knees on the blanket left by Mr. Gribbins. What with the candles flickering merrily away and lighting up the room, it was as cozy a scene as could be imagined.

If only, Robin thought, he did not have to worry ever again about shining shoes!

Chapter XI

A Chilling Customer

The following day, Robin trudged off to spend the day with Mouse. Mouse, having been apprised of Robin's unfortunate attempt at shoe shining while apprenticed to Duck, did not shove any brushes at him unexpectedly. Or, for that matter, shove them at him in any manner at all.

The morning after that, Robin went off with Spider. And although a great deal of instructing was done, by the end of the day, Robin still had not shined a single shoe. Greatly to his relief.

But on the fourth day, his luck ran out.

"You can't go on learnin' the rest o' yer days," said Duck. "None o' us did. None o' us even got friends wot showed us how ter shine. We jist hung 'round someone wot were doin' it, 'til we got arsked ter move on. So time you took a try doin' it on yer own."

There was no escaping it any longer. Armed with his box, brushes, and blacking, and with a fainting heart inside his patched jacket, Robin marched off beside Duck, who was only to help him find a good corner to set up his box. That done, Duck informed him he "were goin' ter do jist fine," then with a wink and a big grin of encouragement, went whistling off to his own place of business.

Unfortunately, he had no sooner disappeared than another shoe-shine boy appeared, older, much bigger, and with tiny pig eyes that looked accusingly at Robin from a red face round as a pie pan.

"Wot does you think yer doin' in my spot?" this individual snarled at Robin.

The terrified Robin, who actually wondered what he was doing in any spot at all, picked up his box and scurried away without a word. It was probable that this spot did not belong to the boy, but the last thing on Robin's mind was to stay and argue about it.

He found another corner two blocks away unoccupied by another shoe-shine boy. But he almost hoped someone would come along and chase him out of this corner as well. Not to mention any other corner he might try. He could then return to the church, probably early, and spend the rest of the day playing with Danny. No one could blame him if he could not find a free corner, now could they? Tomorrow he would try again. Perhaps he would wake up bolder and braver.

But no one came to claim his corner, which must have been a poor choice, because there were no customers either. At least, no one came up to him and said, "Shine, please." Whether any man passing his stand might have been a customer would never be known, for he could never bring himself to chase after one with the words, "Shine your shoes, mister?" He grew paralyzed at even the *thought* of doing it.

Finally, in the late afternoon, a few drops of rain fell. As Robin stood huddled against a wall, they fell faster. Surely no one would be wanting to stand there in the rain having his shoes shined. As soon as the rain let up, Robin determined he would hurry back to the church. The rain lasted only a very short time, but he had already made up his mind to leave. What was the point of standing there damp and miserable when it was clear that he was going to shine no shoes that day? He picked up his box and set off.

All the way he kept telling himself what a failure he was. Visions of the great amounts of money he was going to make had long since vanished. If he continued being a failure, what was he going to do about buying milk for Danny, and the other things he was going to need one day soon? It was hopeless. Just hopeless!

"Blast!"

Robin had just crossed the street to the church corner when he heard this. In front of the church stood a handsome carriage drawn by two sleek horses. The polished brass door handle and the coach lights gleamed in the street lamp near it. A tall, somewhat heavy-set man in a glistening top hat and a black coat richly trimmed in a fur collar, was standing by the carriage and looking down at his feet.

"Blast!" he said again.

Robin started hurrying down the sidewalk toward the back of the building.

"Boy! Boy!" the man called out.

As there was no one else around but the uniformed driver of the carriage up on the driver's seat holding the reins of the horses, Robin stopped and turned around.

"Boy," the man said, "I see that you carry a box. Are you by any chance a shoe-shine boy?"

No stealin', no cheatin', no lyin'. Robin, his heart nearly at a standstill, was ready to forget these promises. But before he could stop himself, he found himself nodding.

"Y-yes," he stammered.

"Well then, don't just stand there," the man said impatiently. "Come on over to the street lamp. It's just come on and should give you enough light to do the job. But be quick about it. My wife is leaving something off at the church and will be right out. Blasted rain! Just enough to leave puddles around for a man to step in when he's got someplace important to go," he muttered.

Robin was certain he was going to keel right over onto the shoes he was supposed to shine. Yet to his surprise, he heard himself saying in a voice cool as you please, "You'd best step over here, sir, and grab on to the post. Keep you steady while I fix up your shoes for you."

Robin could feel the man's eyes fastened on him the whole time he was blacking and shining the shoes. His hands ought to be shaking like a dried leaf on a tree. He knew that. Yet they were as steady as the man's shoe resting on the box. It seemed that St. Something must have been working another miracle. Not a drop of blacking was spilled, nor a scratch put on the shoes. They all but sparkled in the fluttering lamplight.

"That ought to do it, sir," said Robin, giving the shoe on the box a last flick of the polishing rag.

He looked up into the man's face and was glad he had not looked so closely into it before. For he found himself looking past a rich silk scarf, past a black beard, and into dark, piercing eyes, eyes to which no better word fit than the word "cruel." If Robin had not known better, he would have thought he was looking into the eyes of—Hawker Doak!

"What do I owe you?" the man asked.

Robin was so shaken he had all but forgotten he was to be paid. But now the question had been asked, what was he to say? He could suddenly not remember what Duck, or Mouse, or Spider had asked for a shoe shine. Was it two cents? Three?

"Five cents, sir," said Robin in the boldest voice he could muster.

"Here," the man said, carelessly tossing a coin at him.

Somehow, Robin managed to catch it in midair and jam it into his pocket. For all he knew it was no more than a penny.

"Thank you, sir," he said. But he was addressing the man's back, for he had already turned abruptly on his heels and was striding toward the carriage.

Robin snatched up his box, hardly able to get away fast enough. But as he approached the back of the church, he hesitated and then went right on walking away from it. The man was still standing by his carriage, waiting for his wife. They must be people who attended the church, and Robin knew how dangerous it would be for anyone to suspect that the cellar was being lived in by four—no, *five* street boys and a baby.

When he was out of sight of the carriage, Robin stopped a moment under a street lamp and pulled out the coin the man had tossed him. It was *not* the five cents Robin had requested. But it was not one cent either. It was ten cents. Ten whole cents! He could not believe it. For only a few minutes' work, he had earned ten cents. His very first money earned! But what made him almost as proud as the money was that he had done a good job and made not a single mistake. And oh, what a polite and proper businessman he had been! "That ought to do it, sir." "Five cents, sir." There was no doubt in his mind any more. He was going to make a fine shoe-shine boy indeed!

It seemed impossible to believe that he had suddenly gone from having to return with a dismal report of his day, to one quite the opposite. He could hardly wait to report to the boys this amazing news. And while he was at it, why not surprise them with something else as well? It was an idea that had come to him when he saw how eagerly they worked at learning to tell time from his watch. And as he had to wait to get back into the church, why not go right now and get what he needed for the surprise? So that is what he did.

By the time he returned to the church, the carriage had left. But in his shoe-shine box he now carried not only his brushes and blacking, but four pencils and a tablet of paper. Well, they were only pencil stubs purchased from a street peddler, but they would write as well as any new pencil.

Unfortunately, his ten cents had now been reduced to eight cents, as the four pencil stubs had cost him a cent, and the tablet of paper a cent. Two cents out of the precious ten cents he had just earned. But now he knew he could earn it back. And was this not worth every bit of the two cents? For he was going to teach the boys their letters. He would teach them to write their own names.

And yes, he might even teach them to read and write the real name of St. Something!

But as he came bursting into their cellar room with his good news, he found it would have to wait, for there was some other exciting news awaiting his arrival.

Piggy, holding Danny and surrounded by Mr. Gribbins, Duck, Mouse, and Spider, looked up at Robin with an ear-to-ear grin. "Wot kep' you," he said. "Come look. Yer baby brother's done sprung a tooth!"

"Piggy said as how he's been fussin' a bit all day," said Spider.

"I should o' brung 'im a teethin' ring," said Mr. Gribbins. "Hannah done said as how I should. Ain't nothin' she don't know 'bout babbies. I'll be bringin' one t'morrow."

"An' yer Uncle Mouse is goin' ter bring you a rattle," said Mouse.

"Wot d'you mean 'yer Uncle Mouse'?" said Duck. "His Uncle Duck done said it firstest."

It was clear that it was going to be a while before Robin could announce his news. But, in truth, he did not mind a bit. For was Danny's big brother not just as proud of his new tooth as his Uncle Duck, his Uncle Mouse, his Uncle Spider, and his Uncle Piggy?

But when Robin did finally tell them all the events of his day, there was yet more excitement all around. So much so, that Mr. Gribbins found it difficult to tear himself away to go home to his Hannah.

Why then, Robin wondered as the evening wore on, was he not feeling as happy as he should? He had proved that when put to the test, he could be a good shoe-shine boy. He knew now that he really could make money to take care of himself *and* Piggy, and to buy all the milk in the world Danny needed. Further, the boys were just as happy with the pencil stubs and paper and learning their letters, as they had been with learning to tell time from his watch.

So what was bothering him? Why did he have such a feeling of dread? And then, quite suddenly, he saw again the dark, cruel eyes of the man whose shoes he had shined. The leaden feeling he had turned to an icy chill. He almost would have given back the ten cents not to have seen those eyes. Why?

What had the man done but give him ten cents for a five-cent shoe shine? There was really no reason for Robin to feel as he did. No explanation for it. But explanation or not, all he knew was that he did not like the owner of those eyes having anything to do with St. Something. Or anyplace near where he was. And most especially not near his baby brother Danny.

And yet the frightening question remained. Why?

Chapter XII

A Puzzling Report

𝕋

"Wot's ailin' you, Robin?" Duck asked. "You been pickin' at yer supper. You ain't been payin' no 'tention ter wot any o' us is sayin'. Can't be yer biz. You got two customers terday. You got two day 'fore that, an' one day 'fore that. An' there's the ten cents you got off'n that gent outside o' the church. Ain't bad pickin's fer one wot's jist got goin'. Better'n any o' us done when we begun."

"It's not that," said Robin. "It's not anything, Duck. Really."

"Yer lyin'," said Duck, stuffing another bite of bread into his mouth. "C'mon. Say wot's up."

Robin had not wanted to tell them. He had never told them how he felt about that man's frightening eyes, so why tell them about this? Still, that was all in his imagination. This was something else entirely. This was not only frightening. It was very, very real.

"C'mon, Robin. We're waitin'," said Mouse.

"Well," said Robin, hesitating, "it's just that today I saw a friend of my step-papa's. His name is Quill. I met him just before I ran away with Danny."

"So you seed this Quill," Duck said. "That don't mean nothin'. Wot might mean somethin' is if he seed *you*."

"He *did* see me," said Robin. "I know he did, because after I left to come home, he was following me."

At this, all four faces around Robin suddenly froze.

"Did he actual foller you all the way here?" asked Mouse.

"Oh no! No!" cried Robin. "I guessed right away I was being followed, so I turned at the next block and went right on in another direction. I kept on walking and walking. I knew he was behind me, because every time I turned around to look, there he'd be ducking into something. He's thin as a stick. He can hide just about anywhere."

"So how did you git' 'way from 'im?" Spider asked, his eyes ready to pop out of his head.

"I just went on walking," said Robin. "I think he ended up so tired he gave up, because the last time I turned to look, he was gone. But I kept on walking anyway, just to be sure."

"We knowed as how you got home later'n all o' us," said Duck. "But none o' us thought ter arsk why."

"Wot I don't git," said Mouse, "is why he never jist nabbed you on yer corner, if nabbin' was wot he had in mind."

"Maybe he never had nothin' in mind," said Piggy. "Maybe he never 'spected ter see Robin, an' when he did, he jist wanted to see where Robin landed so some other party could go nab him, some other party like maybe his step-pa."

"But even if he don't know where Robin landed," said Spider, "he's seed where Robin does shoe shinin', an' he c'n tell the other party where. That ain't so good neither."

Duck looked around at them, and shrugged. "Seems ter me as how all Robin got ter do is get hisself 'nother corner nowheres near the other one."

"Too bad, seein's how he got this one goin' so good," said Mouse. "We best help find 'im another spot where that boy with the pig eyes an' pie-pan face wot Robin told us 'bout don't come hornin' in."

Going back out into the streets was frightening, but Robin had to agree to what was suggested. After all, he could not stay and hide in the cellar of St. Something the rest of his days.

· · ·

The next day, as planned, a new corner was found for Robin. But before the day was out, Quill had found it as well. Once more he followed Robin when he picked up his box to leave. Up one street and down another Robin went. And though his heart might have been thumping at a great rate, he walked along slowly, carelessly swinging his box as if he were out for a Sunday stroll in the park. He had no intention of letting Quill know that he knew he was being followed. And though Quill followed him longer and later than the first night, once again he finally gave up.

The following day, yet another corner was found for Robin. And the exact same thing happened. But this time, even though Robin led him on a merry chase, Quill stuck with him for even longer than the previous two times. Would he end up following Robin all night, especially when he must realize that Robin knew he was being followed? But what was he hoping to accomplish by this curious game of cat and mouse? Did he think knowledge of Robin's whereabouts could help him get something he wanted from Hawker? That would, of course, mean that Hawker was still looking for Robin, and determined to find him. And that was a conclusion that chilled Robin.

He told it to the boys, and they agreed that he was probably right. It would help if they could find out exactly what Quill was up to, and why. That, however, seemed almost impossible.

"Be nice ter be a fly buzzin' roun' the table wot yer step-pa sits at with this feller Quill," Spider said.

"Wot table were that?" asked Duck. "Robin ain't said nothin' 'bout no table."

"Aw, Duck, why're you allus tweakin' me?" complained Spider. "I jist meant any ol' table. Sometime or other they got ter be sittin' at a table. Ain't that right?"

"That's what they were doing when I met Quill," said Robin. "Spider's right, Duck."

"Yeah, I knowed that. Sorry 'bout it, Spider," said Duck. "But wot was they doin' at that there table, Robin. Guzzlin'?"

Robin nodded.

"Where were that?" asked Mouse.

"A place called The Whole Hog," Robin replied.

"Aint' never knowed o' that one," said Mouse. "My own pa allus goes ter The Rat's Nest."

Suddenly Duck bit his lip and screwed up his eyes. "Wait a bleedin' minute. I'm gittin' a idea here. Spider, I got ter say it come from what you jist said 'bout the fly buzzin' roun' the table. Supposin' it were a *boy* buzzin' roun' that there table 'stead o' a fly. Or maybe jist hangin' roun' nearby."

"Wot boy you got in mind, Duck?" asked Piggy.

"Any one o' us," Duck said. "Robin's step-pa don't know any o' us from spit."

"We don't know Robin's step-pa from spit neither," said Mouse.

"Robin c'n tell us wot he looks like," Duck said. "So tell us, Robin."

"Well," said Robin, "he's big and he has a black beard, and a scar across his cheek. It's from a fight he was in. And he always wears this black jacket."

"You ain't able ter do no better'n that?" Duck asked. "Sounds like a hunnert people wot I know. Wot's 'is name?"

"You mean one o' us got ter go up an' arsk 'im?" Spider asked.

At this, Duck just looked at Spider, shook his head, and sighed. "No, Spider. Wot I were thinkin' is hangin' roun' someone wot looks like wot Robin said. You wait long 'nough, someone's got ter say his name. So wot's 'is name, Robin?"

"It's . . . it's Hawker Doak." Just saying his name made Robin's skin creep.

Mouse's eyes flew wide open. "Hawker Doak! *He's* yer step-pa?" Robin nodded.

"He's the one wot comes 'round collectin' rent where I used ter live with me ma and pa," said Mouse. "I seed him more times'n I cares ter count."

"Do you think as how he seed you?" Duck asked.

"Nah," said Mouse. "They was hunnerds o' kids in the buildin', an' it ain't likely he knowed one o' us. All he were in'erested in were the sight o' me pa's hand forkin' over the money."

"Then sounds like as how yer the one wot gits chose ter do the buzzin' roun' the table at The Whole Hog," said Duck. "You c'n pertend you was there fer yer pa. Ain't nobody goin' ter think nothin' o' that."

"But when is it I got ter go hangin' 'round?" Mouse asked. "I ain't in'erested in hangin' roun' mornin' 'til night. 'Sides, if I'm seed hangin' roun' all day, you think there ain't no one goin' ter arsk questions? Don't take all day ter pick up somethin' fer yer pa."

Duck took a few moments to think this over. "Well, ain't much doubt this here Quill's goin' ter be follerin' Robin agin tomorrow. An' Robin's goin' ter lead him 'roun' again. That right?"

"I believe it is," said Robin.

"So," continued Duck, "soon as Robin knows he ain't bein' follered no more, he high tails it back here. Mouse is waitin' fer 'im, an' *he* hightails it ter The Whole Hog. This here Quill, bein' all wore out from follerin' Robin, more'n likely won't be goin' no faster'n a dyin' rat. So Mouse gits there, sets up his waitin' place near this here Hawker . . . and waits."

Mouse gave a deep sigh. "Sounds as how lots got ter happen 'fore somethin' else happens. An' wot if nothin' happens like wot you said, Duck?"

"You got a better idea?" asked Duck. "Anybody here got a better idea?"

Nobody did.

"Then that's how it's goin' ter be," said Duck.

"Mouse," said Robin, "thank you for doing this. I want to thank all of you. I don't know what Danny and I would have done if . . . if . . . well, I just wish I could get everybody something. When I start making more money, I'd like to get . . ."

"Git us all 'nother one o' them big dinners like you got us first night you b'come one o' us." Duck grinned. "Nah, I were jist tweakin' you. You ain't gittin' us nothin'. Wot Mouse is doin' ain't nothin' he wouldn' be doin' fer any o' us, nor us fer 'im. We all knows as how you'd be doin' the same. So no more 'bout gittin' us anythin'. Did you git that?"

"I got it," said Robin with a sheepish grin.

Mouse need never have worried, for it all happened just as Duck had laid it out. Quill followed Robin. Robin led him the usual merry chase until he gave out. Robin "hightailed" it back to St. Something. Mouse "hightailed" it to The Whole Hog, and then at last raced back with his report to four anxious, impatient boys.

"Wot took you?" asked Duck, even though Mouse had actually returned in little over an hour. This was confirmed by Robin's all-important watch, which had been consulted at least once every other minute. Mouse, fortunately, was too out of breath from running to let Duck know what he thought of the question.

"Did . . . did you see Hawker Doak?" Robin asked hesitantly.

"I seed him," replied Mouse.

"Quill too?" Robin asked.

Mouse nodded.

"Well, wot did you find out?" asked Duck.

"Was . . . was I right, I mean what I was thinking about Quill, and that he might not say anything to Hawker about finding me?" asked Robin.

Mouse stared at Robin for a few moments, and then slowly shook his head.

"Maybe I'd best tell you wot happened from the beginnin', an' you c'n figger it out," he said with a shrug. "You were right 'bout one thing. This feller wot were thin's a stick, like you said, come draggin' in after I done arrived, and I knowed it were Quill. I'd got me a seat nex' from where Hawker Doak were sittin' with a fat man wot I guessed might o' been this Maggot wot you tol' us 'bout. There I sits holdin' this can wot I picked up on the street, lookin' like I were waitin' ter git it filled fer me pa, when this Quill comes in and plunks hisself down like a stone nex' ter Hawker."

"'Hawker, I ain't goin' ter do that no more,' he says. His voice aint' much more'n a whisper an' got a queer little whistle in it. It gives me the creeps, I'll tell you. 'I'm wore ter a bone,' he says, which are a 'orse laugh, 'cause he ain't much more'n a bone anyways."

"C'mon, Mouse, git on with it," said Duck. "Yer killin' us all."

"So Hawker says," continued Mouse calmly, "'You can't quit on me now, Quill. Wot kind o' friend are you? Besides, I'm payin' you handsome, ain't I?'

"'He's doin' that, all right,' says this feller Maggot.

"Then this Quill, he jist grumbles roun' a bit. Then he says, 'Whyn't you jist let me pick him up where he's shinin' shoes and drag 'im back? I think he's on ter me, one night he's goin' ter lead me plumb inter the nex' county. Let me jist pick him up. Why not, Hawker?'

"'I tol' you why not,' says Hawker. 'It ain't him I want. It's the brat I want. The boy c'n go drown fer all I care. You keep follerin' him. One day he's goin' ter let down 'is guard an' lead you ter wot I'm lookin' fer.'

"'Nice thing, Hawker,' says this Quill. 'You git me all wore out, but you still ain't tellin' wot's this all 'bout.'

"'That's right. I ain't. It's my business an' ain't nobody else's. An' now I'm starvin'. I'm goin' home an' git me some grub.'

"So Hawker got up an' went," concluded Mouse. "I stuck roun' a while ter listen ter them two, Quill an' Maggot, goin' on 'bout wot Hawker were makin' Quill do. But Maggot kep' on tellin' Quill wot good money Hawker were payin' 'im, an' if he knowed wot were good fer 'im, he'd shut right on up an' do wot Hawker wanted. Then they upped an' lef'. But Robin, I wanted you sh'd hear all I heerd, so you ain't thinkin' I were makin' a mistake when I said as how I b'lieve you was wrong. It ain't Quill wot's back o' all this. It's yer Hawker Doak!"

"And it's not me he wants," said Robin. "It's not even me and Danny. It's just Danny, my baby brother."

"Why?" asked Piggy, with round eyes.

Why? Robin had no answer to the question. All he knew was that it gave him a terrible feeling of dread deep inside him.

Why Danny?

Why?

Chapter XIII

Pawnshop Revisited

᛭

The next day it started to rain early in the morning. The rain continued all day. It continued the next day. And the next. And the next. It continued to rain and drizzle for six days, and there was no sign that it had any intention of letting up.

There was no use in anyone going out with a shoe-shine box in such weather, for who wanted to have their shoes shined standing out in the wet? And what was the point anyway of having shoes shined only to have them immediately in need of shining again? So while it was true that Robin was freed for the time being of having to escape from Quill, it was also true that nobody, including Robin, was earning any money.

For the first day, and perhaps even the second, it was pleasant to stay in the nice warm cellar and not feel guilty in the least about being there. And now that they had been found out and welcomed by Mr. Gribbins, there were no worries on that score.

The boys played skip rope with an old piece of rope Mr. Gribbins found for them. They played ball in the hallway, courtesy of a ball from the same source. They took turns wheeling Danny all around the cellar in a cart Mr. Gribbins had made for him. And they especially spent a great deal of time with their pencil stubs and pieces of paper, practicing the letters Robin was teaching them. But by the fourth day, they had become restless. And by the sixth, there was a serious worry, for their money supply was dangerously low.

"We shouldn' o' been spendin' all that on wot we was shovin' in our faces," said Spider. "Wot was we thinkin'? Ain't never goin' ter git 'nough fer a proper shoe stan' like we been wishin' fer."

"Look who's talkin'?" said Mouse. "Who's allus wantin' them apples wot ain't got no worm holes? Seems ter me as how it's you, Spider."

"Sorry," said Spider. "But I ain't the one wot wanted ter git that big sausich, now were I?"

"Aw, stop it," said Duck. "Wot's done's done. Blamin' someone ain't gittin' nothin' back. An' ain't we all eatin' nothin' but stale bread now? It's Danny's milk wot we got ter think 'bout. Ain't that right, Robin?"

Robin nodded. It was right, indeed, and he had been thinking very hard about this, and how it had not been very wise to spend so much of his money when he first came. Showing off is what it was. He had only spent two cents later on the pencil stubs and paper, and worthwhile as that was, perhaps he should not have done that either.

"Could we borry from Mr. Gribbins?" asked Piggy.

"Nah, we ain't goin' ter start that," said Duck. "Not 'less Danny ain't got a drop o' milk from anywheres. Mr. Gribbins' Hannah's ailin', and needs lots o' medicine, he says. An' he don't git paid spit, near as I c'n figger. No, we ain't borryin' from him."

"We could borry from the box upstairs," said Spider.

"That ain't borryin'," said Duck. "That's stealin', 'cause wot if we c'd never pay it back? Must be some other way."

"We c'd sell somethin' ter a peddler," suggested Piggy hopefully.

"Like wot?" asked Duck. "Our cups an' dishes we got in the dump? Saucepan from the same place? That'd bring in a pretty penny. An' who'd pay us fer somethin' wot they c'n find in the dump, I arsk you? More'n likely we'd be arsked ter pay fer someone ter take the stuff."

"There's our shoe boxes," said Spider.

"No!" said both Duck and Mouse so sternly, Spider fairly shrivelled away.

"I . . . I could sell my papa's watch," said Robin. "I told you how just before I ran away I had to take money from what my mama left me, to pay Hawker because someone didn't give me all the rent money I had to collect for him. Anyway, before I remembered I had the money, I tried to sell the watch at a pawnshop. Mr. Slyke said he'd give me only twenty-five cents, and I needed fifty, so I never sold it. But I could go back now and get the twenty-five cents."

"Aw, not yer pa's watch!" exclaimed Duck. "That ain't right. You don't want ter do that, do you?"

No, Robin did not want to do that. But twenty-five cents might be just enough to buy enough milk for Danny until they could all get out and start shoe shining again. If there were only something else that he had that he could sell.

The pin and the locket!

When he had taken them from Hawker's drawer, he had considered them useless because they were not money. He had never told the boys about them because they were something he had stolen. But could they not be sold at the pawnshop just as well as the watch? Why had he never thought of this before? And now he might as well come out with it, stolen goods or not, for they were desperate. In for a penny, in for a pound!

"I . . . I have something else I could sell," he blurted.

"Wot's that?" asked Duck.

Before replying, Robin went to where his jacket lay on the floor, reached into a pocket, and pulled out the pin and locket.

"Here," he said, handing them to Duck.

Duck gave a low whistle. Spider, Mouse, and Piggy clustered around him, staring bug-eyed at his hand.

"Wheeooo!" said Mouse. "Where'd you git this stuff, Robin?"

"Stole it," said Robin.

"Wot?" said Spider.

"He said he stealed it," Duck said. "Brush out yer ears, Spider."

"How come you never said nothin' 'bout havin' this stuff?" Mouse asked.

"No stealing, no cheating, no gambling. Remember?" said Robin. "I couldn't tell you about stuff I'd just come from stealing."

"But you ain't said yet where you stealed it from," Piggy said.

"From the drawer where Hawker hid all his stolen stuff. Pins, rings, necklaces—things like that," Robin replied. "Hawker works at the docks, and he collects rents for a landlord as well. But he's in the stealing business too. I don't know if he goes stealing himself, but he's in business with people who do."

"Robbin' from the robber," mused Spider. "Stealin' don't seem so bad when you think on it that way."

"That's right," agreed Duck. "Seems as how yer Hawker were jist gittin' paid back."

"I . . . I guess so," said Robin. "But up until now, I wished I'd never taken anything from that drawer, because I knew if Hawker found anything missing, he'd try all the harder to find me. Then I remembered my mama whispering to me about a locket before she died. I thought she did, anyway, and I thought maybe this was the one, and it might have pictures of my papa and her in it. But it doesn't. I don't know who the people are."

"Mind if I open yer locket?" Duck asked.

"Go ahead," said Robin.

Duck snapped open the locket, studied in a moment, and then brought it up closer to his eyes. "Never seed anyone like the gent b'fore. Lady got the look o' that purty one wot was handin' them dyin' flowers ter Mr. Gribbins first day I come ter St. Somethin'. But this picter's small, and they's probable a million purty ladies jist like this in this picter. Here, any o' you want ter see?"

They all did, so as Duck handed the pin back to Robin, the

open locket was passed from Spider, to Mouse, to Piggy. At last, still open, it came back to Robin. Glancing at it before closing it, he felt his stomach lurch. The pretty lady was still no one he had ever seen. But the man looked like the same one whose shoes he had shined outside St. Something!

Robin looked at it more closely, and then his stomach quickly righted itself. The picture was indeed very small. And while the bearded man in the picture did bear some resemblance to the one Robin had encountered, he no doubt resembled a million other bearded men. No, Robin decided, because he still remembered those cruel eyes, because of his frightening narrow escapes from Quill, and now because of his new fears for Danny, he was once again letting his imagination play tricks on him. No, this picture was just as he had thought before. It was no one he knew.

"So wot does you think yer goin' ter do?" Duck asked.

"Go see my old friend, Mr. Slyke," said Robin.

The weather the next day continued gray and drizzly, and once again there was no setting out to shine shoes. But Robin felt, and the others agreed with him, that he should wait until late afternoon, it being the safest time to go out. Hawker would be at The Whole Hog, no doubt accompanied by Maggot and Quill, who would have no prey to hunt down that day. When the time finally came, Robin set out with high hopes that he would return with enough money to rid them of all their worries.

"Don't let yerself git gypped," Duck said. "Them two pieces is got ter be gold through an' through. Don't let 'im give you none o' 'is cup an' saucer stuff like he done with yer pa's watch."

Yes, Robin was going off with something this time that Mr. Slyke would have to agree was not plated anything! Robin had decided, however, that he would only show him the pin. If he got enough for that, there was no reason to produce the locket, even though he brought it along with him. The locket he would save in case they ever had another emergency; or, if there never was one, to sell and put toward the shoe-shine stand they all wanted. He had great plans indeed for this suddenly realized source of wealth!

The pawnshop was open, as Robin expected it would be, and Mr. Slyke was behind the counter reading his newspaper just as he had been the first time Robin walked through the door. As soon as he saw Robin, a smile almost of triumph appeared on his sallow face.

"Well, I see he's come back," he said, "the boy with the watch. Did you decide to take my offer? I told you twenty-five cents is a good offer. A boy can do a lot with twenty-five cents."

Robin hesitated. With the encouragement of the boys, he had entered the pawnshop feeling quite sure of himself. But Mr. Slyke had a way of making him feel unsure of anything.

"I . . . I didn't bring my watch," he said.

The smile vanished from Mr. Slyke's face. "Then why are you here?" he asked abruptly.

"I . . . I have something else to sell," replied Robin.

The smile halfway returned to Mr. Slyke's face. "What is it? Something else that your papa gave you?"

Stolen from his step-papa was more like it! But Robin did not see that he needed to confess this to Mr. Slyke. He simply pulled the pin from his pocket and laid it on the counter. Mr. Slyke swiftly snatched it up and examined it closely as he had the watch.

"You say you got this from your papa?" he asked, pulling a small magnifying glass from a drawer and looking through it at the pin. He asked the question as if he were simply making conversation and had no real interest in the answer.

"Mmm," said Robin, that passing for either "yes" or "no," however Mr. Slyke chose to take it.

Mr. Slyke laid his magnifying glass down on the counter. "It's gold," he said with a shrug. "But low quality. Diamonds just chips.

Ruby maybe just glass. I can give you one dollar forty-five cents, but I'll be losing money."

"Just one dollar forty-five cents?" repeated Robin, his dreams of sudden wealth instantly evaporating. He had thought at least five dollars.

"Nobody comes to a pawnshop who got a lot of money to spend," said Mr. Slyke. "If I pay you more, I got to charge more, and nobody will look at it. You'd better be smart and take the dollar forty-five cents."

What choice did Robin have? Right now he desperately needed money for Danny's milk. "I'll take it," he said.

Mr. Slyke pulled open a drawer and started to count out money from it. But suddenly he paused, looked stealthily around the empty shop as if there might be someone there listening, leaned on the counter, and drew his face up close to Robin.

"You don't have anything else of your papa's, do you? I'll look at anything you got, but I'll tell you what I'm looking for. This man comes in all the time asking for something that once got stolen from him. He goes around to all the pawnshops hoping someone will bring it in. Now, I'm not saying your papa gave you something that was stolen, but I tell you I look at everything I can because you never know where it came from. This man will pay fifty dollars if it's what he's looking for. Whoever brings it to me gets fifteen, and no questions asked."

"What . . . what is he looking for?" asked Robin.

"It's a locket," said Mr. Slyke, dropping his voice almost to a whisper. "You got anything like that?"

Robin nodded.

"Is your locket round with a small diamond in the middle and roses into it all around?" asked Mr. Slyke. "Locket's got to be gold too. This man's not paying for nickel plate. Your locket gold, is it, with the diamond and roses?"

Robin gulped, and nodded again.

"You got it on you?" asked Mr. Slyke. "Or you got to go get it?"

Robin put a shaking hand inside his jacket, pulled out the locket, and laid it on the counter. Mr. Slyke snatched it up.

"If that isn't what he's looking for, I'll eat it," he said, snapping open the locket. He glanced at the pictures, barely able to contain his glee. "That's him all right. You just might be walking out of here with fifteen dollars more than you thought. Problem is, if you want your money now, I got to go show the man the locket. Won't be gone long. He says any time I get one that fits what he wants, don't waste time getting to him. He says take a cab, and he'll pay for it. You wait here for me to get back."

"H-h-here?" asked Robin.

"Yes, here," said Mr. Slyke, already dropping the locket into his jacket. Then he leered at Robin. "You see, you don't have to worry about trusting me with the locket. I'm trusting you to stay here all by yourself. Now, you could just rob me blind, couldn't you?"

There was something Robin did not like about this plan, especially when Mr. Slyke's trust did not go so far as to leaving the store unlocked and open for business. He hung the "closed" sign on his window, and padlocked his front door, leaving Robin, in truth, a prisoner until he returned. As soon as Mr. Slyke had departed out the back, and Robin heard the sound of that door being locked as well, he began to realize what a ninnyhammer he was. Mr. Slyke could return and say he had lost the locket. Then what? That Mr. Slyke was not above lying, Robin was certain. But he could do nothing about it now, and just resign himself to waiting.

Examining everything in the store was interesting enough, but a person can only examine trays of tarnished teaspoons, stacks of mismatched dishes, torn old prints, and other similar items so many times without getting weary. Time dragged, and every time Robin consulted his watch, it seemed that only two or three minutes had passed. But at long last Mr. Slyke appeared from the back of the shop. He seemed nervous, but still gave Robin a smile displaying a full set of large, yellowed teeth. Taking down the "closed" sign, and unlocking the front door, he hurried behind the counter.

"Come here," he said, his smile broadening. "I've got something for you."

Mr. Slyke honest after all! Eagerly, Robin went to the counter and waited as Mr. Slyke opened the money drawer and rattled coins around in it. He was making so much noise, that Robin never heard the front door to the shop open. But suddenly, he saw something dangling from over his head before his eyes. It was the locket Mr. Slyke had taken with him.

"Waitin' for somethin', were you, boy?"

Robin whirled around, and found himself looking into the glaring, enraged eyes of Hawker Doak!

Chapter XIV

Peril Under the Pier

🔱

"Thought you were the clever one, didn't you?" Hawker's eyes narrowed to malevolent slits as he grabbed Robin by the collar. "Well, let me tell you somethin', boy. You got to get up pretty early in the mornin' to put one over on Hawker Doak. Runnin' off like you done. *Stealin'!* I found out you were a thief when Kringle paid up his fifty cents. You never went back to get it from him like I ordered you, you chicken-livered little weasel. You got it from my hidin' place under my bed, which you must o' found out from spyin'. Good thing I weren't stupid enough to tell him I already been paid.

"Knowin' you stole money led me to checkin' my drawer you and your ma was told to keep your noses out o'. And guess what I found out? You been thievin' in there too. And I supposed as how you believed I was never goin' to track you down. Ain't that a fact? Come on, answer me. Ain't it?"

As this was an impossible question for Robin to answer, he did not answer it. For that he was shaken so hard by the collar that his teeth rattled.

"Thanks for your help, Slyke," Hawker said. "If it's all right with you, I'll be back to settle my account with you later. Right now I got to be goin', because I got more business with this little thief."

"Before you go," said Mr. Slyke, "you wouldn't like to check his pockets, would you? I had to leave him here alone while I went for you, if you get my meaning."

"I get it, all right," said Hawker. He started shoving his hand roughly into one pocket after another of Robin's jacket. "So what've we got here?" he said, holding up Robin's watch. "Where'd you steal this from, you bloody little thief?"

"I . . . I . . . I didn't steal it," Robin blurted out.

"So you didn't steal it, eh?" Hawker said, sneering. "Then where did you get it?"

"It was my papa's," said Robin.

"Funny, I never seen it," Hawker said. "Hidin' it from me, eh? Well, you just gave it to me, boy. And here's what I'm goin' to do with it." He threw the watch on the counter in front of Mr. Slyke. "What'll you give me for it, Slyke?"

Mr. Slyke picked up the watch and examined it as if he had never seen it before. "Fifteen cents," he said, without so much as the flicker of an eyelash.

"I'll take it," said Hawker, holding out his hand.

Mr. Slyke handed him some coins from his drawer, and Hawker jammed them into his pocket without even looking at them. "Now you just come with me, boy."

Dragged by the collar, Robin stumbled with Hawker from the pawnshop into the street. As soon as they were out of the sight of Mr. Slyke behind his pawnshop window, Hawker slammed Robin against a brick wall.

"All right, boy," Hawker said from between clenched teeth. "Now you're goin' take me to where you been holed up all this time with the little brat. You got that?"

"But . . . but I don't have him with me," said Robin, his voice trembling.

"Don't try to make a fool out o' me, boy, or you'll come to wish you'd never been born," said Hawker. "You can't tell me you never took him with you when you run off."

"Oh, I . . . I *did* take him, Hawker," said Robin. "Remember how he was crying the night I left? You told me to keep him quiet or get him out of there. So I took him for a walk."

This honesty stopped Hawker for a moment. Then he pulled Robin away from the wall by the shoulders, and slammed him back again.

"I told you not to make a fool o' me, boy. Think I'm stupid, do you? Well, here's stupid for you. Stupid is tryin' to tell me you took the brat for a walk when all his stuff was missin' with him. You think I'll buy that?"

"All right," said Robin. "I . . . I guess I have to tell you. I was running away with Danny. I . . . I saw how you were going to hit him, and I thought . . . I thought you didn't want us around any more."

"You're breakin' my heart," said Hawker. "But snivelin' ain't goin' to get you anywhere, boy. And so far you ain't answered my first question. Where you hidin' the little brat?"

For this question, Robin needed another St. Something miracle. Did miracles extend to providing someone with a lie? Well, for this kind of lie, apparently yes!

"I . . . I walked a long time because I didn't know where I was going," said Robin. "Then I began thinking maybe I was wrong about everything, and I'd better just go home. But by then I was so tired I sat down on a step in front of a building to rest. Danny was asleep by then, and I . . . I must have gone off to sleep for a while too. When I woke up, Danny and all this things were gone. I was so scared, I went on walking away, and never came home. It's what happened, Hawker, honest."

"You're lyin'," said Hawker.

Some moments passed as they stared at one another, Hawker menacing, Robin quaking.

"I'd kill you, boy," said Hawker. "But I expect you know

somethin' you're not tellin'. And dead you ain't any use. So your life is now spared. But one thing you'll be showin' me, and that's where you're holed up. And you'll be showin' me right now."

"Now?" Robin felt as if he had been slammed against the wall again.

"Now," said Hawker, grabbing him by the collar once more and marching him down the street. "You lead the way, boy."

And just where was Robin going to lead him? The only place he knew he was *not* going to lead Hawker was to St. Something. Other than that he did not have the wildest idea in the world. But miracles from St. Something seemed to be falling on his head like raindrops. For as he started walking, he suddenly did have an idea—the pier where the boys had lived before they found their new home! He had never been there, but they had given him a good description of where it was, and he was certain he could lead Hawker right to it.

The only thing he now needed to pray for was that none of the boys who had shared the pier with his friends would be "at home" when he and Hawker arrived. They, of course, would not know Robin, and what then? Robin's brain, by now all but completely paralyzed, could not come up with an answer to that. It was still early enough, however, that the street boys were still out there *in* the streets. So all that was needed was for the space under the pier to look lived in, but with no boys in it.

Robin was able to find the pier with little difficulty, but when they went under it, he found that his luck had run out. For by the light of a single fluttering candle, a ragged young boy, who looked like any one of the hundreds who roamed the streets, sat cross-legged on the ground gnawing on the tag end of a chunk of bread. He looked up as Robin arrived with Hawker, but went right on chewing without saying a word.

"This the place?" Hawker asked Robin.

"Y-yes," stammered Robin.

"You know this boy?" Hawker addressed the boy on the ground, jerking his head at Robin.

Standing frozen at Hawker's side, Robin managed to nod his head so slightly it was almost no nod at all. Probably only a street boy, schooled in the art of signalling, would have caught it.

"Sure," said the boy, chewing away with his mouth open.

"Live here, does he?" asked Hawker.

Robin nodded again.

"Sure he lives here," the boy said, appearing more intent on picking something crawling across his bread than answering Hawker's questions.

"What's his name then?" Hawker asked slyly.

The boy looked at Robin for a signal. Of course, getting none, he mumbled something unintelligible.

"What was that?" Hawker shot at him. "I didn't get it. Say it again."

"It's Jocko," the boy said, giving Robin a helpless shrug.

"Well, it ain't. So what do you think of that?" said Hawker, pouncing on this gleefully.

"It *is* Jocko," Robin burst out, finally locating his voice. "It's my street name. You remember how Maggot said when I got out on the street, I'd have to change my name for protection. Well, that's what I did."

This had the desired effect of stopping Hawker. But after mulling it over and being unable to find any loopholes in this reply, he came up with another thought.

"Did he have a brat . . . a baby with him when he first got here?" he asked the boy.

Robin quickly shook his head.

"Baby?" said the boy. "Yer crazy, man. Who'd be bringin' a baby here? We got trouble ter spare carin' fer usselves. Wot we want with a baby?" Then the boy grinned at Robin. "You stayin' or leavin' fer the evenin', Jocko?"

"He's leavin' with me," snapped Hawker.

"Jist askin'," said the boy.

As they had been talking, Robin had been digging into his jacket pocket, and managed to find something Hawker had missed in his earlier search. It was a one cent piece. As they turned to leave, Robin managed to flip the coin in an underhanded throw, and turn his head enough to see the boy catch it expertly and stuff it in his pocket. With another grin, he tipped his cap at Robin.

Robin was learning to like these street boys more and more. This one had saved his skin. He only wished he had had more to give, but he had to be satisfied knowing that the cent would buy the boy another chunk of bread.

As for Robin himself, what was to happen to *him?*

"Where are we going now?" he asked Hawker.

"You're goin' to your old home, boy," snarled Hawker. "Where did you think?"

Chapter XV

A Good Boy

⚜

R obin was now Hawker Doak's prisoner. He had seen Hawker remove the key from the inside lock, making certain, of course, that Robin had seen him doing it. And there had been a final click of a key turning in the lock outside when Hawker had gone out again. Oh yes, Robin was now his prisoner. Hawker left no doubt about that. It seemed that Robin was being guarded like one of Hawker's precious stolen jewels.

Yet had Mouse not heard Hawker saying Robin could drown for all he cared? It was Danny he wanted. So, perhaps, like the spider who weaves his web to catch his prey, Robin was to be the web meant to catch Danny. But how? And when? All Robin knew was that Hawker made no further mention of him. It looked as if he had forgotten Danny altogether.

Instead, Robin continued a prisoner, himself the prey caught in Mr. Slyke's cleverly woven web. And he was not only a prisoner in the apartment, but when he left it as well. For he was always in the company of Hawker, who never took his eyes off Robin for a moment.

Robin felt desperate. How was he ever to get word to the boys of what had happened to him, or find out from them if Danny was all right? As several days went by, this began to seem more and more impossible. And then one day, as he was going with Hawker to collect the rents, there was Mouse coming right toward them swinging his shoe box!

What was Mouse doing there? Robin knew Mouse was dangerously near his old neighborhood, and if caught by his pa, might well have a whole new crop of welts and bruises on his thin body by evening. Could Mouse be out scouting for Robin and not worrying about his own safety? But what if he spotted Robin and, without thinking, ran up to him before even noticing that Robin was with Hawker? Then, known to be Robin's friend, might Hawker not cleverly have him followed by Quill, who could be led right to Danny? Much as Robin wanted to talk to Mouse, he must warn him away. Carefully, Robin lowered his hand to his side, and made a fist. Would Mouse understand that this time it meant danger, stay away?

Mouse, with a blank look on his face, drew closer and closer. He was soon so close that Robin could see the freckles on his nose. But what was that curious blinking he was doing with his eyes, looking up and down at a furious rate. Robin followed his eyes down, and there saw it—the fist matching his own at Mouse's side!

It had all taken place in one heart-stopping moment. Mouse, without so much as a muscle twitching on his face, had passed them right by, and was gone. But he knew! And now they would all know that Robin was back in Hawker's clutches and was his prisoner. There was nothing they could do to rescue him, any more than he could find a way to escape. But Robin knew he would at least sleep a little better that night, now that the boys knew what had happened to him.

There were actually times when Robin was not locked in the apartment and was out of Hawker's sight. That was when he, Robin, was collecting rents in the dark, dank halls of the buildings Hawker managed, while Hawker himself sat outside waiting. But unless Robin could come up with a way of climbing out the window of one of the apartments, there was no escaping any building but through the front door.

It was the same, day in and day out. No one to talk to except Hawker, growling, grunting, snapping, or snarling at him. And still no mention of Danny. But Robin had to believe Hawker was up to something. He was certain of it. And the prospect was frightening. Then one day something happened that added to his fears.

He always dreaded collecting the rents, and dreaded even more finishing the job, coming out, and seeing the hulking body of Hawker Doak waiting for him at the side of the stairs. But one day he came from a building to find Hawker missing, not sitting in his usual place. Instead he was standing beside a carriage and horses that had stopped outside the building and was talking to a strange man. The man caught sight of Robin as soon as he stepped through the door, and said something to Hawker, nodding his head in Robin's direction.

"Get over here, boy!" Hawker commanded him. "And be quick about it." He had a sound in his voice Robin had never heard there before. It was a kind of nervous fear.

Robin ran over to the carriage, looking up at Hawker and waiting for his next instructions. But it was the man who spoke.

"Look up at *me,* boy," he snapped.

And Robin found himself once again looking up into the cruel, dark eyes of the man whose shoes he had shined outside the front doors of St. Something! Eyes that now seemed to be piercing Robin's brain as he studied Robin's face curiously with narrowed eyes.

"Do you shine shoes?" he asked abruptly.

Robin had no choice but to nod. After all, it was what Quill had found him doing for a number of days, and there was no reason to think it had not been reported to Hawker.

"Then are you not the boy who shined my shoes for me outside St. Katherine's Church some days ago?" the man asked.

"No, sir. I . . . I don't know where that is," replied Robin, praying that the man's eyes were not actually able to see into his brain, or could hear his heart pounding in his chest. For St. Katherine's Church was, in truth, no other than St. Something!

The man continued studying Robin's face. "I don't often make such mistakes," he said. Then he added as if it were an indifferent afterthought, "You're not a boy given to lying, are you?"

"N-no, sir," replied Robin, hoping his face did not betray him, which he felt was what the question was supposed to accomplish. It otherwise made no sense, for who in their right mind would have answered "yes" to it?

"All right, boy," Hawker said roughly. "You wait for me on the steps until I finish talkin' with Mr. Highcrofft."

When Robin had left them, the men continued talking in low voices. Mr. Highcrofft appeared agitated and angry. And as he walked back to the apartment with Robin, Hawker was sunk in deep silence.

The following afternoon, Robin was not taken out with Hawker, but was left locked in the apartment. When the supper hour came, as announced by the chipped enamel clock sitting on the kitchen counter, there was nothing to prepare for a meal, because the kitchen cupboards were empty. The food brought in for Robin, who was naturally not allowed out to buy any for himself, was as little as Hawker felt obliged to provide just to keep him alive. So Robin stayed hungry most of the time. He would only have something to eat that evening when Hawker returned home.

But it was not too much longer before Hawker came stamping through the front door. And he was smiling! Or at least what passed for a smile with him.

"Well, now we got a treat for supper tonight," he said. "It's cake with real sugar frostin' on it. And I'll sit down and share it with you b-b . . . Robin."

Cake? Sharing? *Robin?* Was Hawker ill? Was his mind gone? What was this all about? Robin could not even begin to guess, and he could not see himself asking Hawker to explain.

Hawker's attempt at making conversation as he sat stuffing the larger portion of the cake into himself was purely laughable.

"How was your day?" he asked Robin.

"It . . . it was fine," replied Robin, whose day had been as dull and dreary as always. But should he now ask Hawker how his own day was? Was it expected? "H-how was *yours?*" he finally blurted.

"Good," replied Hawker, his mouth so full of cake the crumbs were spilling out. "Hey, you know somethin'? If you keep on bein' a good boy like you been doin', I'm givin' some thought to sendin' you back to school. How'd you like that, eh?"

"I . . . I . . . I would, thank you," the stunned Robin managed to reply.

Hawker then stood up, putting a welcome end to the conversational attempt. "All right, I'll be thinkin' more about it," he said, giving a swipe across his mouth with his shirt sleeve. "Now I'm goin' out. See you go to bed and get your rest."

Robin was too startled by this last expression of interest in him even to reply. But Hawker, undoubtedly up to his neck with being pleasant, stumped out and slammed the door in his usual manner. That did not bother Robin one bit. His stomach wonderfully full of cake, all he could think about was that there might not be a factory in his future after all. Only school! And freedom! If only that freedom would come soon enough for him to somehow make it to St. Something, his friends, and most especially—Danny.

The following day, however, although Hawker remained as pleasant as was possible for him to be, he still left Robin locked up in the apartment. And he left something else as well, the jewelry drawer wide open, and a pile of money sitting in full view on top of the chest of drawers. As Robin already knew where the jewelry and money were hidden, what was this all about? Was it to serve as a strong temptation for Robin to help himself to whatever he wanted? And why?

Then, that evening, after Hawker had come home with more food for Robin than usual and was leaving again, he turned to Robin and said, "Well, I told you, you been bein' a good boy, never tryin' to run off again or nothin' like that. Now I see how honest you been. No money gone. No more lockets and pins missin'. So," he paused to see how this was settling with Robin, "tomorrow maybe you can come out with me, and I'll see to lettin' you off the hook a little. What do you think of that?"

"I wouldn't mind," said Robin. Would not mind? His heart was racing so fast he thought it would burst right out of his chest.

But Hawker had no sooner left than he began thinking over what had just been said. And he decided that Hawker was either very stupid or very clever. "Never tryin' to run off," he had said. Well, how could Robin run off anywhere, being either locked up or, but for rent collecting, never out of Hawker's sight? As for taking money or jewelry, did Hawker think Robin such an idiot as to take anything at all of his, and then sit there in the locked apartment waiting for him to return and find out about it? It must have been some sort of test that put him in no danger of losing his money or the jewels. But why was Hawker suddenly being so nice to Robin? What was behind it?

And then it came to him. Clever Hawker might be, but not so clever that he knew a certain conversation—one he had had with his friends Quill and Maggot at The Whole Hog—had been heard by a certain friend of Robin's. Mouse! In Mouse's words, Hawker had said, "One day's he's goin' ter let down his guard an' lead you ter wot I'm lookin' fer."

Let down his guard! That was exactly what Hawker was working toward—Robin letting down his guard. He must never have believed Robin's tale of Danny being kidnapped while he, Robin, sat on the steps sleeping. But why did all this niceness start right after Hawker's meeting with that man, Mr. Highcrofft? There was no question that Hawker had been sunk in unhappy thought after the two men had met. What was Mr. Highcrofft's connection to all this? But most of all, why had Robin had that feeling of dread when he looked into the man's eyes, not once, but twice?

This was not only more puzzling. It was more terrifying. Robin knew that he was now going to have to be more careful than ever. Oh yes, very, very careful indeed!

Chapter XVI

A Final Wish

🔱

"Get your coat on. You're comin' with me," Hawker said to Robin in the late afternoon of the following day. "Today's the day I'm gonna let you off the hook. Just a bit o' a try out, you might say. And no monkey stuff, or the deal's off. You get my meanin'?"

"Oh yes!" said Robin eagerly. But he knew exactly what Hawker was up to.

"Off the hook." There was no "off the hook" about it. Robin had the hook imbedded in his throat as much as any poor fish caught in the ocean. And Hawker was just as carefully playing out his line with Robin at the end of it. As for "no monkey stuff," why that was exactly what he really wanted, just being clever in warning Robin against it.

Where they headed when they left the apartment was, not surprisingly, Hawker's great entertainment center, The Whole Hog. And there, also not surprisingly, were Quill and Maggot waiting for him.

"You remember my friends Quill and Maggot here," said Hawker jovially when they arrived at the table where the two were sitting. "Say 'hello' to the boys, Robin."

"Hello, sirs," he said politely.

"Ain't he the little gentleman? He'll go far, I tell you," said

Hawker, winking at the two men as they exchanged grins. "And such a good boy too, that I'm lettin' him off the hook for a while tonight. But just for a hour. A boy can go visitin' a lot o' places in a hour. Sorry about losin' your pa's watch for you, Robin, but here's mine for tellin' when the hour's up. See how I'm trustin' him now, boys, with my own watch?" The still grinning "boys" nodded together like two toy monkeys on a single string. "Now you go along, Robin," Hawker said, waving him off. "And mind you . . . a hour! Next time, maybe it'll be for longer."

Dodging the crowded tables and chairs, Robin made his way back to the front door. But as he went, he managed to turn his head slightly so he could still see the table where the three men were sitting. And with no surprise he saw Quill sliding from his seat. He was going to be following Robin again! Well, Robin knew exactly what to do about *that*.

Strolling at the slowest possible speed, stopping at every single store window and staring into it for minutes on end, he paraded up one side of the street, and down the other, consulting Hawker's watch at every gas lamp. An hour was an hour, and he had no intention of going one minute over it.

The whole time he was parading up and down the street, Robin was quite aware of Quill darting in and out of stairwells and doorways right behind him. Once, Robin darted into a stairwell himself, enjoying seeing Quill, passing it, frantically looking for him. If this whole game were not so deadly, Robin could have been having a good time. And of course, he had the pleasure of imagining Quill's disgust at having Robin return promptly to The Whole Hog after having chased him no place but up and down the street.

But Hawker had no intention of giving up, and so the next late afternoon, the same game took place. And the third afternoon as well. Robin wondered how long these chases would continue before Hawker would give up and accept that Robin might have been telling the truth, and really did not know where Danny was.

Then what? Would it mean returning to the old cruel treatment and being imprisoned again? Would it mean no school, but going into a factory instead? And would he ever find a way to escape to St. Something? To the boys? To Danny?

Then on the fourth afternoon, just as the street lamps were being lit, with Quill still dogging his footsteps, Robin was startled to see Maggot running toward them. Quill stepped out of the shadows to meet him. No longer making any pretense of hiding, the two men ran toward Robin. They were both panting, their eyes glaring, and their faces pale as dough.

"Come with us!" Maggot said, gasping for air. "Hawker's in terrible trouble. There's been a fight. He's been took to your home. He's askin' to see you."

"B-b-but how did it happen?" asked Robin, feeling his knees grow weak under him.

"Can't use my breath talkin'," said Maggot. "You'll find out soon enough. But we got to hurry. From what I seen, there ain't much time left. And you got to show us the way to your home, boy, 'cause we ain't never been there before."

Not much time left! Something terrible had happened to Hawker, the last thing in the world Robin would have thought of, or even wanted, much as he wanted to get out of Hawker's clutches. But no questions were to be answered until they reached their destination. Numb with shock, he could only lead Quill and Maggot in deadly silence down the streets toward what gave every promise of being a grim and terrible scene.

When they arrived at the apartment, they found the front door open, and beyond it only the dim, fluttering light of a single oil lantern set on a table. Robin quickly led them through that front room into the one beyond it. There they found three men standing up, leaning against the wall, all staring at the man stretched out on the bed. The light of a single oil lamp flickered over an ominous rose red stain that had spread its awful bloom across his chest. The stain was a curious match to the livid gash that cut across the ghastly white skin under the man's closed eyes. The man on the bed was Hawker Doak.

Robin, not knowing what to do, remained standing helplessly beside Maggot, who spoke to one of the men.

"He should o' been took to the hospital," Maggot said.

"You was there," the man said. "You heard him. He said he wanted to come here. Said he'd bring hisself if none o' us would do it. Kept sayin' he wanted to come here to talk with the boy."

"Anyone thought o' gettin' a doctor?" asked Maggot.

"Fish's gone lookin' for one," said the man. "Don't know where he's gonna find one, but won't do much good anyhow. If you ask me, Hawker's a goner. I think he's just keepin' hisself alive till he sees the boy."

Just then a terrible groan came from the figure on the bed. Maggot gave Robin a shove toward it.

"Go on over there, boy. You're what he wants."

Trying to overcome his horror, Robin hesitantly approached the bed.

"It's . . . it's me, Robin, Hawker. I'm . . . I'm here."

Hawker finally opened his eyes.

"Glad they could find you," he said. His voice was so weak and hoarse it could barely be heard. He looked across the room at the men all staring at him and Robin. "Boys," he said, struggling to raise his voice, "thanks for bringin' me here like I wanted. You're good lads, the lot o' you. But no need to stay on. Quill and Maggot'll stay here with me. But right now, I'd like if you two would wait outside for a minute. I got somethin' to say to the boy here."

"Hope to see you back at The Whole Hog soon, Hawker," one of the men said as they all filed uncomfortably from the room.

As soon as the men had left, Hawker attempted a weak grin. "They're lyin', and they know I know they're lyin'. They know my number's up and they ain't ever gonna see me back at The Whole

Hog again. But now, Robin, there's somethin' I want you should do. It's got to be done quick, because I ain't got much time left. You go over to my chest there and look inside the top drawer that's alongside the one where I keep all the other stuff you know about. In that drawer, there's money, there's a name and address on a slip o' paper, and there's the locket you had. What I want is for you to take a cab with the money, take along the locket, and go to the address what's on the slip o' paper. You give the locket to the man with the name you see on it. No other man! You give him the locket, and you say him who sent it is dyin' and got to see him—urgent."

"What if he won't come?" asked Robin.

"He'll come all right," said Hawker, groaning with pain. "He'll come. Just you hurry. And tell Quill and Maggot they can come back. They'll stay with me till you get back. But hurry, boy! Hurry!"

Robin had never been in a cab in his life. He had no idea even how to go about getting one. Chase one down, he supposed. But he had to go three blocks before he even found any to chase. And when the cab drivers saw that it was only a boy in a patched jacket waving them down, they passed him right by. Valuable minutes were lost before a cab driver finally stopped long enough for Robin to wave a wad of bills in his face.

The cab driver gave a low whistle when he saw the name and address on the slip of paper Robin handed him. "Sure this is the place?" he asked.

"Yes," said Robin, climbing into the cab. "And please hurry!"

"Yes, *sir!*" said the driver.

Robin had jammed the slip of paper into his pocket with the money and the locket. He had never even looked at it. Where was he going that had so impressed the cab driver? Now with nothing to do but listen to the *clop, clop* of the horses' hooves, Robin looked at the slip of paper the cab driver had returned. The small oil lantern outside the cab door gave just enough light for him to read it. The address meant nothing to him, but when he saw the name above it, he wanted to fling open the door and leap from the cab. For the name on the slip of paper was Highcrofft. Mr. Jonathan Highcrofft!

Robin's blood froze. He had no real reason for hating the man, but he did. He had no real reason for being afraid of him. But he was. *Clop! Clop! Clop!* The horses' hooves drummed on. But Robin knew he would do nothing to keep them from moving ahead. After all, he was carrying out a man's wish. A man's final wish!

Clop! Clop! Clop! The horses' hooves drummed on. And on.

Chapter XVII

A Terrible Confession

When the cab finally pulled to a stop at the address given on the slip of paper, the cab driver saw fit to whistle again. For they had come to a splendid brick house, a house which more properly could have been called a mansion. Robin had guessed that Mr. Highcroft was rich, but he could never have guessed as rich as this. It only added to his fright after he paid the cab driver and was walking up the steps to the enormous double, oak doors. Robin's hand was trembling when he pushed the brass button that made chimes ring deep inside the house. Almost instantly, it seemed, the doors opened to reveal a tall man dressed in a swallow-tailed coat and striped trousers. The look on his face made it clear he was not pleased to find a boy in a patched jacket standing at the door.

"What is it you want?" he asked stiffly. "If you're here begging, we can't help you." He paused a moment. "Well, if it's food you want, and you're hungry, go around to the back door. There may be something they can give you there."

"I . . . I . . . I'm not begging," stammered Robin. "I've come to talk to this person." He handed the man, clearly the butler, the slip of paper from his pocket.

"Step inside then," the butler said, his face expressionless. "I'll go see if Mr. Highcroft is able to see you."

Robin stepped into a great, high-ceilinged entry hall, its two sparkling crystal chandeliers lighting up a grand, curved stairway rising up one side, two tall mirrors, and at least four large oil paintings framed in elegant, carved gold frames. This was a room that did nothing toward making Robin feel more comfortable. It was well that he had but a few moments to stand there quaking before Mr. Highcrofft appeared from the drawing room. But this was not the Mr. Highcrofft Robin expected to see!

Oh, this man had a family resemblance to the other. There was no denying it. But although he did indeed have a black beard, his face was somewhat thinner. And his eyes! They were a bright blue, with a gentle, kindly look to them. These were not the eyes Robin had seen before.

"You may go now, Fletcher. I'll take it from here," he said. Then he looked down at Robin. "Who is it who sent you, young man?"

"Mr. Hawker Doak," replied Robin.

"Then this is a mistake," was the quick reply. "I don't know the man, but my cousin Franklin Highcrofft does business with him. Mr. Doak must have made a mistake with this. I'm Mr. Highcrofft, all right, but Mr. Jonathan Highcrofft as is written on this slip. I don't know how he got this name and address. Do you?"

Robin shook his head. "All I know is he said he only wanted to see the man whose name is on the slip, and no other. And he told me to give you this." Robin pulled out the locket and handed it to Mr. Highcrofft.

Mr. Highcrofft's face paled when he saw it. He opened the locket, staring silently at the pictures in it. "Where did Mr. Doak get this?" he asked.

"I . . . I don't know," stammered Robin.

"Is the man your father?" asked Mr. Highcrofft.

"No, my step-papa," replied Robin. "But he's been in a fight, and he's dying. He wants you to come as quickly as you can."

"Wait here . . . what is your name, young man?" asked Mr. Highcrofft.

"It's Robin," he replied.

"Well, wait here, Robin. I shall be right back. Fletcher!" Mr. Highcrofft shouted as strode back into the drawing room. "Have the carriage brought round to the front door. And very quickly, if you please. *Very* quickly."

Only minutes later, Robin was back in a carriage, listening once again to horses' hooves drumming, hooves carrying him back to where Hawker Doak lay dying in his bed. Perhaps already gone, for all Robin knew. And the man beside him, Mr. Highcrofft, might have been thinking the same thing. His hands were tightly clenched and his face grimly set.

"Are you sure, Robin, you know nothing about where this locket came from?" Mr. Highcrofft pulled himself up from deep thought to ask.

"No, sir," said Robin. "I . . . I'm sorry."

"That's all right," Mr. Highcrofft in a kindly voice. "I'm sure if you knew anything, you'd tell me."

After that, he retreated back into his deep thoughts, and they rode the rest of the way in silence.

As soon as they arrived at their destination, Mr. Highcrofft ordered his carriage to wait, and he ran with Robin to the apartment.

"Is he . . . is he . . . ?" Robin asked when they entered Hawker's room.

"Still with us," replied Quill.

"But fading fast," added Maggot. "Good thing you're back."

Upon hearing their voices, Hawker opened his eyes. "You brought Mr. Highcrofft with you, Robin?" he gasped. "Have him come by the bed. Quill and Maggot, I'd be pleased if you'd step out of the room whilst I talk private with these two."

As the two men left, Robin approached the bed with Mr. Highcrofft. He could see the locket tightly clutched in Mr. Highcrofft's hand.

"Mr. Highcrofft," Hawker said, his voice now so weak they had to lean down to hear him, "I'm doin' what I'm doin' because I'm dyin' and want to make things right with my Maker before I go. I've been a bad man, Mr. Highcrofft. Been terrible to this boy and to his ma. Ain't that right, son?"

"It doesn't matter now, Hawker," Robin said, not knowing why his eyes should suddenly fill with tears on hearing this man who had indeed treated him so cruelly now call him "son." "What I remember is how you got me that good cake. Remember?"

Hawker tried to smile. "It *was* good, and it was nice eatin' it together. But it's to Mr. Highcrofft I got a terrible confession to make. You got the locket, did you, Mr. Highcrofft?"

"I have it," he replied, holding it out in his hand. "But where did you get it, man?"

"Stole it from your wife's room in the hospital when she was havin' her baby," replied Hawker. "It was right by the crib."

"I guessed it," said Mr. Highcrofft, a catch in his throat.

"But there's more," said Hawker. "And it's much worse. The same night your wife was havin' her baby, my wife was havin' hers. It was the baby already on its way when I married her and became this boy's step-pa."

"But why are you telling me all this?" asked Mr. Highcrofft. "You have already explained how you came by the locket, so precious to me because of the photograph in it of my dear wife, as well as my own. It isn't necessary for you to say more, and you are very weak. This is taking a lot out of you."

"I'm tellin' you because it got to be told," moaned Hawker. "Because what happened is that my wife's baby was born dead . . . yours was born alive. And I got paid a lot o' money to switch them that same night. How I did it is no matter. I did it.

Robin, your brother was never your real brother."

Danny never Robin's real brother!

"Did Mama know?" gasped Robin, his head reeling.

"No way she could o' not known about her own baby not bein' born alive. So I had to tell her, only she never knowed whose baby was put in her own baby's place, or where it come from. But I told her she better not say a word about any o' it, or it'd be your life." Hawker's voice faded into silence after this grim admission.

"But who put you up to this, man?" asked the stunned Mr. Highcrofft, finally able to speak. "Who was it paid you a lot of money to do this terrible thing?"

"It was Franklin Highcrofft," replied Hawker.

"*Franklin? My cousin?*" breathed Jonathan Highcrofft, his face contorted with shock and disbelief. "Why? *Why?*"

"He never told me why," replied Hawker, his voice barely above a hoarse whisper. "And I never asked why. I just wanted the money. But he said he didn't care if the baby never lived. If it did, he'd take care o' sending it someplace where no one here could ever find it. But he wanted to know, always, where it was."

"Then tell me," Jonathan Highcrofft cried out, "where is our baby now? Has Franklin already taken him and sent him away? Please, I beg you, you must tell me."

"I don't know if he is alive or dead," replied Hawker, now struggling for every breath. "The baby got stolen, but not by Mr. Highcrofft. Had me searching high and low for it, afraid some-one'd find out the story and would take it back where it belonged."

"Stolen? You mean kidnapped? How did it happen, man? How? Please, can't you tell me more?" pleaded Jonathan Highcrofft.

But in reply, Hawker only gave a terrible groan. His head rolled over, and he was gone. Gone into another world, never to speak in this world again, nor ever answer another question.

"May God have mercy on his soul," said Jonathan Highcrofft.

Then tears suddenly streamed down from his eyes, and he threw his face into his hands. "Oh God!" he sobbed. "Our baby! Found only to be snatched away again. And where in this big, cruel city have we any hopes of ever finding him? Oh, please let me wake from this nightmare! Our baby, alive but gone!"

Then Robin put his hand gently on Mr. Highcrofft's shoulder, shaking with his sobs. "I know where your baby is, Mr. Highcrofft," he said.

Chapter XVIII

A Supper Invitation

🔱

"St. Katherine's Church! And hurry!" said Jonathan Highcrofft to his driver as he and Robin climbed back into the carriage. "I would dearly love to stop by home first," he said when he and Robin were settled inside. "I know my wife Adelaide is anxiously awaiting what news I have to bring her about the locket, which of course I showed her before I left the house. Yet think of the other news I'll now be bringing her as well! But I want to make certain our baby is indeed alive and well before I see her. You say he's been named Danny?"

"Mama let me choose the name," said Robin. "His name is Daniel, but we always called him Danny."

"We'll have to see how that sits with Adelaide," said Jonathan Highcrofft. "For the moment he'll certainly remain Danny. Oh, I still can't believe this! Our baby alive and all this while cared for under the floorboards of the very church our family attends. Why, I even serve on the church vestry! So far, though, Robin, I know nothing of how he came to be there, for indeed you've not had the chance to tell me. So please now, you must tell me everything you can. Every last thing!"

So Robin did, starting with describing the dread baby farm run by Mrs. Jiggs, where Danny was put by Hawker after Robin's mama died. He told of how he had seen Hawker Doak's deadly hand raised against Danny just as it had been raised against Robin himself, and how he feared for Danny's life. That, in the end, he said, was what caused him to run away. For running away, no matter how difficult it would prove to be, would give Danny a chance to live and not face almost certain death at the hands of Mrs. Jiggs and Hawker Doak.

Robin even told how he was, in desperation, going to leave Danny on the steps of St. Katherine's Church, hoping someone would take him home and care for and love him as Robin did. And that was when he discovered the boys living in the cellar of the church. Asking nothing in return, they had taken in Robin and Danny. They had become a family, Robin said. Piggy, who could not work because of his bad leg, stayed home to look after Danny, while the rest of them went off to shine shoes.

"They're all Danny's uncles now," said Robin. "Uncle Piggy, Uncle Duck, Uncle Spider, and Uncle Mouse. And oh, Mr. Highcrofft, I hope nothing bad will happen to the boys now they've been found out. I don't want them to have to go back to living under the pier, or sent back to a pa that beats them just as Hawker beat me."

"Robin," said Jonathan Highcrofft, "turn and look at me. I promise you nothing bad will happen to those boys. You have my word on it. What exactly will happen to them you must give me a little time to think about. But please don't tar me with the same brush as my cousin Franklin. What kind of monster would *I* be to turn on these boys who have without doubt helped you keep my baby son alive? I can only hope that the baby is still as you left him." Jonathan Highcrofft paused to clench his fists and struck the seat beside him impatiently. "Why isn't this carriage going faster? How long did you say since you'd seen my baby?"

"I . . . I'm not certain," replied Robin. "I lost track of the days. It might be as long as two weeks. But Mr. Gribbins will . . ." Robin stopped and threw a hand to his mouth. He had never intended to say anything about Mr. Gribbins' part in all this. It might cost him his job!

But Jonathan Highcrofft was quick to pick up on the name. "Mr. Gribbins? Was he in on all this?"

"He ... he found us out," replied Robin, for it was too late now not to confess. "It was when he heard Danny crying for his milk. He likes us being there because he likes the company, he says. He says he was a street boy once too, and thinks they should be treated better than rats. And he loves babies. Please, Mr. Highcrofft, nothing bad will happen to Mr. Gribbins either, will it? His Hannah's been ailing, and he doesn't have enough money even to buy her medicines that she needs. What will he do if he loses his job at St. Something?"

"Robin, look at me again," said Jonathan Highcrofft. "Believe me, Mr. Gribbins is not going to lose his job. I don't know about his wisdom in storing boys in the cellar of the church, but I certainly can't fault his reasons for doing it. But far from losing his job, I think it's high time he had a salary raise, a *big* one. He's been a loyal and faithful servant to the church, and there's no excuse for this not having been taken care of sooner. Did you say Hannah's been ailing? He's never said a word about it. I'm sorry to hear it, and you may be sure we'll look into what kind of care she's been getting, and see that she has everything needed." Jonathan Highcrofft paused as a puzzled look crossed his face. "St. Something? May I ask where that is, or even *what* it is? I thought we were talking about St. Katherine's?"

At last, Robin had a reason to smile. "We *are*. St. Something is just what the boys call it. They can't read or write, so they can't read the sign in front of the church. But they say all the churches they know about are called St. Something or other. So St. Something is what they call this one."

Jonathan Highcrofft produced a boyish grin. "Well, St. Something certainly had a secret hiding in its cellar, that's all I can say. Five boys and a baby!"

He leaped from the carriage almost before it had come to a stop in front of the church. Robin could barely keep up with him as he raced to the cellar door. His hands were trembling as he pulled out a ring of keys from his pocket.

"Good thing I'm a vestry member," he said. "Always have the church keys with me. Never know when they'll be needed."

"Mr. Highcroft," Robin said, hesitating, for he knew how anxious the man was to see his baby for the first time, "would . . . would it be all right if I went into the room first? I don't want to scare them by us both coming at once."

"Of course! I've let my excitement run away with me. You go on in first," Jonathan Highcroft said, lowering his voice to a whisper as they entered the hallway. "I'll wait here and give you a few minutes."

So he remained behind as Robin crept softly to the door through which he could see the faint light of the candles he knew must be burning. When he entered the room, the boys did not see him at first, for they were all down on the floor, laboriously writing on scraps of paper with their pencil stubs. Robin cleared his throat, and Piggy looked up.

"Robin!"

They were all on their feet in an instant, crowding round him.

"We been dyin' here, wonderin' wot were happenin' ter you," Duck said.

"How'd you git away?" Mouse asked.

"C'mon tell us. Tell us!" Spider started jumping up and down in a high state of excitement.

But before Robin could answer a single question, Jonathan Highcroft, having heard the uproar from the room, could contain his impatience no longer. He ran into the room.

The boys' faces froze.

"Wot did you do, Robin? Lose us our home?" Duck asked simply.

"Do we got ter go back ter the pier?" Piggy asked.

"Or git sent back ter our pa?" said Spider, his pale face grown even paler.

"Or the workhouse?" said Mouse. "Wot you done ter us, Robin? We b'lieved as how you was our friend."

Jonathan Highcrofft, to his great credit, restrained his desperate desire to see what it was he had come there to see. He quickly replied for Robin, who was too stunned to speak.

"Robin is still the very best friend you could have," he said. "And I have made him a solemn promise that not one of you is going back to live under the pier, or to fathers who beat you, or even to the workhouse. Just what we're going to do about finding you a new home, as I told Robin, you must give me some time to work out. But I'll stake my life on it that you'll be going to a kind of life you can't even have dreamed about. And now, please, I'd like to see my baby son. Is that he asleep over there in the corner?"

Before anyone had a chance to reply, Jonathan Highcrofft was striding to the nest of rags on which Danny was sound asleep. He dropped to his knees. In a moment, his shoulders began to shake, for he was sobbing uncontrollably.

"Wot's he talkin' 'bout?" asked Mouse, still with a wary look on his face despite the assurances from Jonathan Highcrofft. "Yer pa's dead, Robin, an' Danny's yer baby brother. Don't make sense ter me."

"You never kidnapped him nor nothin', did you?" asked Spider.

"Aw, wot would he go an' want ter kidnap a baby fer?" said Duck. "Use wot brain you got, Spider, an' think 'bout it."

"Anyone wot's goin' ter tell it ter us?" asked Mouse.

"I will later," Robin said. "I promise. And everything else as well."

Piggy then walked over and tapped Jonathan Highcrofft on his shoulder. "Danny jist had his evenin' feedin' o' milk," he said. "Oncet that happens, he's out like a bleedin' little light. You c'n pick him up an' never hear no peep out o' him."

Jonathan Highcrofft leaned down and picked Danny up as if

he were made of spun glass. Tears were still rolling down his cheeks as he stared at the baby.

"Yes, he's a Highcrofft all right. There's no mistaking it. But I hope you will all understand that I want to take him home to my wife at once. You'll hear the whole story from Robin later, but I want you to know now that until tonight, I didn't know our baby was alive. My wife still doesn't know. And Robin, I want you to come with me, for there are many things I want to settle tonight, late though the hour is getting to be. But I want to thank you boys for what you have done. And again I make my promise that your lives will only change for the better, and you have nothing to fear."

Then suddenly, through his tears, Jonathan Highcrofft managed to produce a boyish grin. "Come to think of it, we might even start that change tonight. What, by the way, did you boys enjoy for supper this evening?"

"We didn't enjoy nothin'," said Mouse. "We had our usual o' stale bread."

"Don't fergit water," Spider said. "We had that, too."

"And that was it?" said the disbelieving Jonathan Highcrofft.

"Split up an apple," said Duck, giving it further thought.

"An' the worms in it," Spider said, wrinkling his nose.

"Well," said Jonathan Highcrofft. "Mrs. Beckett, our cook, prepared a roast chicken for my wife and me tonight. When she does a chicken, she always does two so we can enjoy it for our luncheon the next day. I'm sure she won't mind planning something else for us. So, how would you boys like to come with Robin, Danny, and me, and dine on roast chicken? If I'm not mistaken, there were some roast potatoes left. And, oh yes, a cake with cream layers and a very good frosting."

"Choclit?" asked Spider, his eyes popping.

"I believe so," replied Jonathan Highcrofft. "A very rich, dark chocolate, if I'm not mistaken."

Needless to say, when he climbed back into his carriage,

delirious with happiness, he not only had his baby and Robin with him—and an old cloth shopping bag filled with diapers, bottles, and a tiny tin spoon and bowl, which Piggy had insisted he must take along—but four awestruck boys crowded on the front seat across from him.

Chapter XIX

A Vile Crime

🔱

As soon as Jonathan Highcroft, carrying Danny, had let himself into his home with the five boys at his heels, four of them goggle-eyed at seeing this elegant room for the first time, he rang the bell for his butler. Fletcher appeared almost before the bell had stopped ringing.

"Here, Robin," Jonathan Highcroft said, handing him the bundle that was the peacefully sleeping Danny. Then he peeled off his hat and coat and handed them to Fletcher. "Fletcher, is Mrs. Highcroft still in the drawing room?" he asked.

"Yes, Mr. Highcroft," replied Fletcher, who as a perfect butler never allowed his expression to change when he saw the friends his employer had brought with him.

"Well, then," said Jonathan Highcroft, taking Danny back from Robin, "would you please escort these young men out to the kitchen, and ask Mrs. Beckett to sit them all down at the kitchen table, and allow them to have all they want of that second roast chicken I know she has prepared. Any potatoes and other vegetables she has left from supper may also be served. And please remind her that they're to have as much of that cream cake with the chocolate frosting as they can cram into themselves.

"I'll want some time alone with Mrs. Highcroft. Then I'll ring and ask you to deliver some urgent notes to my cousin Franklin and my grandfather. After that, I'll want you to escort this young man"—he pointed to Robin—"into the drawing room. As for you other fellows, if you don't mind, I'll ask you to remain in the kitchen for a while after Robin leaves you, until I call for you. You can entertain Mrs. Beckett with stories of stale bread, and worms in apples, and all the rest. I've little doubt she'll find that very interesting!"

What Fletcher thought of the ragged guests he was escorting through the house was certainly never revealed in the rigid expression on his face. It is possible, however, that when he saw one slack-jawed guest roll his eyes and punch another guest in the ribs, the faintest smile might have passed over his face. There was no way, of course, that this phenomenon could ever be confirmed.

When Robin was finally summoned to the drawing room by Fletcher, he found Adelaide Highcrofft sitting on a settee with the baby in her arms, and Jonathan Highcrofft standing before her gazing down at them in a clear state of wonderment. Both still had eyes brimming with tears.

"This is Robin, the young man who saved our baby's life," said Jonathan Highcrofft.

"And for which, if we spent our lives doing it, we could never thank you enough," said Adelaide Highcrofft, her soft, sweet voice a perfect accompaniment to her gentle face.

"The boys helped save him too," said Robin, determined that they should have all the credit due to them.

Jonathan Highcrofft smiled at him through his tears. "I've already reported about his Uncle Piggy, who was such a good nursemaid while you went to work, and his Uncle Duck, and Uncle Mouse, and Uncle Spider, whom you shall soon be meeting, Adelaide. We have no words to express our gratitude to them. But it's you, Robin. It's you, son, who was most responsible for saving him from what was almost certain death."

There it was again—that word "son." But Robin was nobody's son. And now he no longer even had a baby brother. He now had no one. Danny was most miraculously going to belong to just the kind of family Robin had wanted for him. And this was not a family who had simply picked him up off the church steps, but was his *real* family. Only that real family did not include Robin. Suddenly, it was all more than he could bear. He threw his arm over his face to hide the fact that he was crying bitterly.

Immediately, he felt an arm thrown around his shoulders. "What is it?" asked Jonathan Highcrofft. "What's wrong?"

"D-D-Danny's not my little brother any more," sobbed Robin.

"Oh, my dear child!" Adelaide Highcrofft cried. "What are you talking about? Of course he's still your brother. No blood bond is needed for that. What has made him your brother is caring for him and loving him as much as you have."

"And that doesn't even begin to address the fact that you saved his life," said Jonathan Highcrofft. "What could make him more your brother than that, son?"

Robin then raised his eyes to look into Jonathan Highcrofft's own. "Oh Mr. Highcrofft, sir, you should not call me that. I'm not your son. I'm no one's son."

"Jonathan, you may tell him," Adelaide Highcrofft said swiftly.

"You're quite certain?" her husband asked.

"Absolutely," she replied. "Without any reservations."

"All right then," said Jonathan Highcrofft. "Robin, your mother and father are gone. So, now, is your stepfather, such as he was. Before you joined us, I spoke to Adelaide about something, and it seems that she agrees with me. I realize we've only just met you, but I believe myself to be a good judge of character. I think you're a fine young man, and we'd both be proud to have you in our family, to carry the name of Highcrofft, and to be our baby's true brother in every sense. I don't think he could have a finer big brother. Is this something you'd like?" Jonathan Highcrofft gave Robin a searching look. "Would that by any chance be a smile?"

"Of course it is, Jonathan!" said Adelaide Highcrofft. "And I believe we have our answer. Now for goodness sake, hand Robin your handkerchief so he can wipe his eyes and won't be spilling tears all over his baby brother when he comes to sit beside me."

She held out an arm to welcome to her side a Robin whose tears now could only be called tears of joyful disbelief. For who could have ever thought that his plans to leave Danny on the steps of a church would ever have such a happy ending?

But Robin had no sooner dropped down beside Adelaide Highcrofft and his baby brother, than the doorbell was heard to ring.

"Robin, I must warn you that what is about to take place might be a fairly ugly scene," Jonathan Highcrofft said. "But I need you here, as you will see."

"What do you mean by 'ugly scene,' Jonathan?" his wife asked quickly. "What could possibly be ugly about Grandfather and your cousin coming here to be told the joyful news of our baby son?"

"There is more to it than that, my dear," said Jonathan Highcrofft. "When I first brought the baby to you, I wanted to spare you the whole story at that happy moment. You don't have to stay for it now, if you don't wish. You can hear it all from me later."

"Of course I want to stay," said Adelaide Highcrofft without hesitation. "If this meeting concerns our two sons, of course I want to be here."

"As you wish, my dear," said Jonathan Highcrofft as Fletcher ushered two men into the room. "And Fletcher, please close the drawing room doors, won't you?"

Of the two men who had entered, one was a distinguished elderly gentleman who stood as straight and tall as the younger man beside him. The younger man, though bearing a strong family resemblance to the older man and Jonathan Highcrofft, was heavier set and with piercing dark eyes rather than the gentler blue of the other two. They were of course the eyes of Franklin Highcrofft, and Robin stiffened when he saw their owner.

"Good evening, Grandfather. It was nice of you to come at this hour. You too, Franklin," said Jonathan Highcrofft.

"Your note hardly gave me any choice, nor probably Grandfather either. Harriet was not too happy about my being dragged out at this hour, I can tell you. What's this all about, Jonathan?" Franklin Highcrofft snapped.

But then suddenly old Mr. Highcrofft beamed. "Is that a baby in Adelaide's arms? Why, what a crafty pair you are! Adopting a baby and no one knowing about it." He quickly strode over to where Adelaide Highcrofft sat beside Robin, holding Danny. "No, no, dear, I won't wake the baby. I just want to look at it. Is it a boy or girl, Adelaide?" he whispered.

"A boy," she whispered back.

"Crafty, indeed, Jonathan," said Franklin Highcrofft. "But an adopted baby certainly doesn't meet the terms of the agreement. Isn't that right, grandfather?"

Old Mr. Highcrofft finally took his eyes off the sleeping baby. "No, no, no, of course not, Franklin. But there's hardly a need to bring that up now."

"I believe there is, Grandfather," Jonathan Highcrofft said. "For the baby is *not* adopted. He is the son born to Adelaide."

"What? Why? How?" stammered old Mr. Highcrofft.

"Why don't you ask Franklin?" said Jonathan Highcrofft, looking steadily at his cousin. "I believe he can tell you all about it."

By now, all blood had drained from Franklin Highcrofft's face. It had become nearly as pale as his elegant, starched collar. But he must have been studying Robin all along, for now he swiftly raised an accusing finger at him.

"What is that boy doing here?" he asked coldly. "And what has he been telling you? I know him. He's Hawker Doak's stepson, and a born liar. You can't believe a word he tells you, Hawker informed me. I myself tested him. I asked him if he were the boy who shined my shoes for me outside St. Katherine's, and he point blank denied it. Said he didn't know the place. But I'm not stupid or blind. Of course, he was the boy!"

"I . . . I had to lie!" Robin cried to Jonathan Highcroft. "When I was at St. Katherine's, Hawker was having me followed every day. It was his friend Quill who was doing it. I knew he was, and I led him every which way, but never near St. Katherine's until I knew he'd given up. If Hawker ever found out it's where I went after Quill stopped following me, he would have guessed that my baby brother was somewhere near there and searched every building to find him. I had to lie!" Robin's voice broke. "I had to!"

"And there's the grand liar for you, Franklin," said his cousin. "He lied to save the baby from his wretched stepfather. I'd buy a bushel of such lies if they ever came on the market. But are you going to tell Grandfather what part you played in all this, or should I?"

"You might as well," Franklin Highcroft replied with an indifferent shrug. "Why not, if it gives you any pleasure."

"It gives me no pleasure, Franklin. I can promise you that much," said Jonathan Highcroft. "But first I must tell you that what I have learned did not come from Robin, the 'born liar,' as you choose to call him. Hawker Doak is dead, Franklin. He was in a fight and, as he lay dying from a fatal wound, he sent for me. You must have given him my name and address in the event you were needed for business dealings you had with him, and could not be located. In any event, I was with him when he died. Shall I go on, Franklin?"

"Be my guest, Jonathan," he replied coolly.

"All right, then," said his cousin. "Apparently Hawker Doak had a deathbed conversion, as they call it. I'm sure he committed a great many sins in his life, but this one weighed most heavily on his soul, and he was able to make his confession to one of the people he had most injured.

"It seems that his wife gave birth to her baby son at the same time and in the same hospital where Adelaide gave birth to *our* baby. You may recall, Grandfather, that we had arranged for her to be there rather than at home, on the recommendation of her physicians. How Hawker Doak did the deed, he wouldn't say, but he somehow managed to exchange his baby, dead but a few minutes after birth, with our baby."

"The poor, distraught man!" said the anguished Adelaide Highcrofft. "So desperate to have a baby he could do such a terrible thing."

Her husband shook his head. "No, Adelaide, his baby was probably one he never wanted. It was to be another stepson to him, another burden on its way before he had even married the baby's mother. I couldn't bring myself to tell you the whole truth when I brought our baby to you. But the exchange was made purely for money, money paid him by my cousin Franklin."

"Franklin!" Adelaide Highcrofft threw a hand to her mouth to hold back a cry of horror.

"Is this then the 'part' you say Franklin played . . . instigating this act of madness?" old Mr. Highcrofft asked, his face a picture of revulsion. "But why would he do such a thing. *Why?*"

"Can't you guess, Grandfather?" asked his grandson. "*I* have. It's that miserable vow you made, already referred to by Franklin . . . the vow made in writing, mind you, that whichever one of your two grandsons produced the first male heir to carry on the blessed Highcrofft name . . . spelled with the two f's you loved informing us when we were growing up . . . would inherit all your extensive tenement holdings."

"God help us!" exclaimed old Mr. Highcrofft. "Is that what's at the root of all this?"

"I believe it is. Am I right, Franklin?" asked Jonathan Highcrofft.

"If you say so," returned his cousin.

"The irony of it is," continued Jonathan Highcrofft, "is that I've never wanted those blessed tenements. Great Scott, doesn't this family have enough wealth as it is? I told you I didn't want them many a time, Grandfather. Before Mother and Father died, they often heard me say I never even wanted to go near those places. It's why Franklin took them over when he lost his own parents and you needed someone to run them for you. That misery and wretchedness doesn't seem to bother him."

"Oh, what have my pride and stupidity brought me to?" groaned old Mr. Highcrofft. "I've always known you had a dark streak in you, Franklin. But heaven help me, I never thought you capable of anything so vile as this. All because of greed. Your greed and my stupidity. Greed and stupidity! What a wonderful combination!"

"Not just because of greed on my part," Franklin Highcrofft hurled back. "You may attribute more of this to retribution, if you will. Give me credit for that. Or perhaps you've forgotten that Jonathan stole from me the sister I always wanted."

"He couldn't steal something from you that you never had, Franklin," said his grandfather coldly.

To this, Franklin Highcrofft merely shrugged. "Well, there's something else. This whole thing was an accident of fate, you might say. In some incidental conversation we had, Hawker Doak mentioned that his wife was ailing, and the doctor held out little hope for the child she was to bear. That birth was to happen about the same time as Adelaide's baby was due. I also knew they were to be in the same hospital, although, of course, Adelaide was to be in a private suite in another part of the hospital, while Hawker Doak's wife lay in a public ward.

"I then simply began thinking 'what if.' At first it was more wishful thinking than anything else, at one stroke not only to acquire the tenement holdings, but to avenge myself. I spoke to Hawker Doak, who assured me he could manage the exchange without my name ever coming into it, presuming all fell into place. It did, much to my surprise. I never really expected it. As you can see, however, this was certainly not something I'd plotted and planned for months or years. Whatever that's worth."

"For your information, it's worth exactly nothing, Franklin," the outraged old Mr. Highcrofft flung at him. "There's not one thing you can say to justify such a heinous crime no matter what you dig up to add to your despicable list. Not a thing!"

"Then I won't even try," said Franklin Highcrofft. "I'm sorry I disappointed you, Grandfather. I apologize. But what are you going to do about this, Jonathan? I suppose you'd like to see me hanged."

"Right now, yes, I would," replied his cousin. "Thrown behind bars for the rest of your life at the very least. Of course, I haven't had much time to think about it, but so far this is what I've concluded. First of all, though Grandfather may have been at the root of this madness, he had nothing to do with perpetrating this unspeakable crime. He's proud, even if overly proud, of the family name, and I won't have it besmirched by having you taken to court and thrown in jail. Furthermore, I don't wish to see Harriet, your innocent wife, and also Adelaide's sister, with a jailbird for a husband. And most especially, I don't wish to have our son's cousin, Harriet's expected child, to have a jailbird for a father."

"It's not that I wish Franklin behind bars, much as he deserves it, as you say," said old Mr. Highcrofft. "But surely you're not letting him off without some kind of retribution for this hideous act, are you, Jonathan?"

"I do have an idea, if you'll go along with it, Grandfather," his grandson replied. "First, I'd like you to destroy those papers in which you leave your tenement holdings to the grandson who produces the first male heir."

"Consider it done," said old Mr. Highcrofft.

"What I'd like you to do then is turn those holdings over now, half to Franklin and half to me, if you're willing to do that," said his grandson.

"I'm perfectly willing," said old Mr. Highcrofft. "But I thought you never wanted the tenements, Jonathan."

"I didn't," he replied, "not as they are, at any rate. But as soon as I get the buildings, I intend to have them torn down and rebuilt. No human being should have to live as those poor wretches do, worse than rats in a sewer. My intention is to put up decent buildings in their place. And my suggested punishment, if you want to call it that, for Franklin, is that he must do the same with his share of the tenements. And lest there be any misunderstanding, I want you to make that a condition of your gift of the buildings to us *both,* even though you can have no doubt as to what *my* intentions are."

"I suppose I need to thank you for this, Jonathan," said Franklin Highcrofft. "So, thank you. But what I want to know is what you plan to tell the world and all our friends about the sudden reappearance of the baby. And what am I to tell Harriet?"

"I'm sure Adelaide and I will simply tell the truth, Franklin," replied his cousin. "And that is that the villain who kidnapped our baby confessed to the deed on his deathbed, and the baby was returned to us. I see no need to say more. If you choose to tell Harriet the same, we will abide by that. Outside of this room, whose doors I requested be closed, all are dead who know anything of the whole truth. I'm certain I speak for Adelaide, Grandfather, and the young man with us, Robin, when I say that, but for the explanation as I've given it, everything remains locked with those of us here. But now I fear it's getting late. Harriet will be growing concerned and looking for your return, Franklin. Grandfather, I'd like it if you could remain for just a few more minutes."

"No need to call Fletcher. I'll let myself out," said Franklin Highcrofft.

"Oh, there is something I wondered further about," said Jonathan Highcrofft. "Weren't you concerned about doing business with someone like Hawker Doak? He could have held you in his clutches the rest of your life, blackmailing you, Franklin."

"I'd thought of that," said his cousin, "but it would always be his word against mine, wouldn't it? And which one of us do you think the courts would believe? I must say, though, the possibility of a deathbed confession never crossed my mind. Well, good night, all. I'm happy to see the baby is doing well."

"Strange coming from you, Franklin," said Jonathan Highcrofft. "Didn't you tell Hawker Doak you didn't care if he died?"

"No, no, no, he got that quite wrong," was the cool reply. "What I said was that if the baby should die, I would not hold him responsible. That's all. Well, good night again!"

Chapter XX

An Invite Accepted
⚕

"This is very hard for me, Jonathan and Adelaide," said old Mr. Highcrofft, "being the one responsible for setting these horrible wheels in motion. What you two must be feeling is beyond my powers to imagine."

"Well, I have to say my feelings would be far different if I weren't sitting here holding this precious baby, Grandfather," said Adelaide Highcrofft. "As it is, all I can feel is a profound gratitude for having him come back to us."

"I'm glad to hear you say that, my dear," said old Mr. Highcrofft. "Nonetheless, what Franklin has done is past belief. You're being very good to him, I must say, Jonathan."

"And I've explained why," returned his grandson. "But I'd also like to think of the good that's coming from this terrible incident in our lives. I'm thinking about the new buildings that will be going up to replace those miserable tenements, Grandfather, and about the poor wretches who will be given the chance to live a decent life because of the new buildings. But we'll talk about all that later. Right now I wish to introduce you formally to Robin, who is the one who saved your great-grandson's life. Robin is going to join our family, Grandfather, and we intend to put the legal wheels in motion immediately so that he will very soon become a Highcrofft, and our baby's official brother. Robin, shake hands with your soon-to-be great-grandfather."

Robin quickly ran to shake the hand of the old man who was smiling warmly at him. "Pleased to meet you, sir."

"And I, you," said old Mr. Highcrofft. "But as to saving the baby's life, I believe there's a great deal missing in this story that I haven't yet been told."

"There is, Grandfather. A great deal!" said Jonathan Highcrofft. "But because of the late hour, I'd like to ask, if it's all right with you, that we put off telling the whole story until tomorrow."

"I'll try to be patient," said the old man. "But one thing you can at least tell me is what you'll be calling this baby of yours."

Jonathan Highcrofft sent Robin a twinkling glance. "You mean we haven't mentioned it? Why, his name is going to be Daniel, although of course we'll be calling him Danny. It's a name both Adelaide and I like very much."

"And well you should!" said Danny's great-grandfather. "After all, you have at least four ancestors with that name."

"I didn't know that," said his grandson with a contrite grin. "I don't suppose there's a Robin stuck away in there someplace, is there?"

Old Mr. Highcrofft laughed. "Actually, I believe there is!"

"What fun!" said Adelaide Highcrofft. "You wouldn't look it up for us, would you, Grandfather?"

"With pleasure!" replied the old man.

"But now, Grandfather," said Jonathan Highcrofft as he went over to ring the bell, "another reason for asking you to stay on a while was not just to meet another great-grandson, but to be introduced to the four young boys who probably made it possible for Robin and Danny even to be here at all, isn't that right, Robin?"

"Oh *yes!*" he replied, so fervently there could be little doubt his whole heart was in his reply.

"Fletcher, would you be kind enough to bring in the four young gentlemen now in the kitchen?" Jonathan Highcrofft asked his butler, who had now arrived.

And it was but a few minutes before Fletcher returned with his small parade of boys, who, now filled with roast chicken and cream cake, came jauntily through the doorway, only to freeze into four stone statues as soon as they entered the grand drawing room. Only their round eyes moved, roaming around the room until they happily lighted on something they knew, Robin and Danny.

"Grandfather," said Jonathan Highcrofft, "I'd like to introduce you to Danny's Uncle Piggy, his Uncle Duck, his Uncle Mouse, and his Uncle Spider. I'm sorry I still don't know which is which, but Robin, would you like to do the honors?"

Robin went over to the boys, and with an enormous grin on his face, held a hand over each boy's head as he put the right name to it.

"I want you to know, Grandfather," said Jonathan Highcrofft, "that these boys, who all ran away from homes where their fathers beat them on a regular basis, used to live under a pier. I still have to learn how it was accomplished, but they recently took up residence in the cellar of our church."

"You mean St. Katherine's?" asked the astonished old man.

At this point, it suddenly beecame too much for the boys to stand by with their mouths hanging open listening to someone tell their story.

"We calls it St. Somethin'!" Duck burst out.

"And where did that name come from?" inquired the curious senior Mr. Highcrofft.

"We ain't able ter read n'r write," said Mouse. "So we wasn't able ter read the sign wot's in front o' the church. But most churches wot we knowed was St. Somethin' or other, so St. Somethin' 's wot we called the one we was livin' in."

"I see," said old Mr. Highcrofft, who was now resting his chin on his folded hands and staring at the boys with a bemused expression on his face.

"But Robin were teachin' us our letters 'fore he got caught by

Hawker," said Spider. "We been practicin' 'em whilst you was gone, Robin."

"Only thing we never done were finish sewin' our clothes like you was doin'," said Piggy. "You done sich good work, none o' us wanted ter sperl it."

"But one thing we done, Robin, were start *worshin'* our clothes. You might o' seen as how we was lookin' cleaner," Spider said. "Weren't easy doin' it, cause we ain't got no changes, but we done it."

"Duck's put it in them promises we made ter the Landlord," said Mouse. "Now it's no lyin', no cheatin', no gamblin', *an'* keepin' clean."

Jonathan Highcrofft exchanged a puzzled look with his wife. "What's this about a landlord?" he asked. "Robin never got around to telling me about that."

Duck jerked a thumb upwards. "Him wot's Landlord o' the church," he said. "I said ter Him if He'd leave us stay there, it's how it were goin' ter be with us. We ain't never gone back on them promises neither. An', Mr. Highcroff', you said as how you'd be fixin' ter git us 'nother place ter go. I'm sayin' ter you now, any-place we go, we'll be keepin' them promises."

"I'm glad to hear that, Duck," said Jonathan Highcrofft. "Well, Grandfather, I think you can see the cut of these boys."

"I can indeed," the old man replied.

"At any rate," Jonathan Highcrofft continued, "one of the reasons I wanted you to meet these young men was not just because I wanted you to know who had taken in your baby great-grandson and his brother, nothing asked of them, and probably saved their lives. But you have a very creative mind, and I thought you might be able to help me find them a new home as I promised them I would do. I think you can understand why, now that I know about it, I can't let them continue living in the church cellar. But I'm certainly not going to have them sent back to live under a pier, or to fathers who beat them, or even, heaven forbid, to the workhouse."

"Did you have anything at all in mind, Jonathan?" asked his grandfather.

"Nothing," he replied. "But among all your friends I don't suppose you could think of anyone with a big house that has eight or so bedrooms in it, and a heart as big as the house, who might consider taking in these splendid young fellows, do you?"

Old Mr. Highcrofft shook his head. "Not in a million years, I'm afraid. That's a very big order, Jonathan. Why, I have a house with the eight bedrooms you suggest, but I wouldn't even think of—"

"Well now, Grandfather," interrupted his grandson. "Adelaide and I were rather hoping you'd mention those eight bedrooms."

Old Mr. Highcrofft threw up his hands. "Oh, no, no, no! Now I'm beginning to see where this is all going, and I tell you it's not possible. I couldn't even begin to consider it."

"Why not, Grandfather?" said his determined grandson. "You've been rattling around in that mausoleum ever since Grandmother died. You don't even entertain any more. Mrs. Delbert has been complaining she doesn't properly earn her housekeeper's pay, nor do any of that army of servants you have there. Whom, I might add, you won't let go because, though you'd never admit it, you do have a very big heart, Grandfather."

"But four boys!" he groaned. "Have you no mercy, Jonathan?"

"None in this case," replied his cold-hearted grandson. "Oh, and Grandfather, did I forget to mention your seven-bedroom 'cottage' in the country, and at the shore your—"

"Enough! Enough!" moaned old Mr. Highcrofft. "You have made your point. And to think I let myself be led right into this. I've always prided myself on being a fairly crafty fellow, but you've certainly beaten me at my own game. Well, all right then, but how do we know these boys would even want to come and live with an old codger like me?"

Jonathan Highcrofft laughed aloud. "Old codger indeed! You're younger than most men half your age. And having these boys around will make you younger yet. Anyway, boys, do you or do you not wish to go and live with this old codger?"

"We ain't never been arsked," replied Duck.

"Well then, for heaven's sake, I'm *arsking* you," grumped old Mr. Highcrofft.

"Wot we usual do 'bout most stuff is hold a meetin'," replied Duck. "But don't think we need a meetin' fer this. We accepts yer invite."

"When do you think they could come to me, Jonathan?" asked old Mr. Highcrofft, who looked rather as if he had been struck on the head with a very hard instrument.

"Why not tonight?" replied his heartless grandson.

"But don't they at least need to return to the church to pick up their belongings?" inquired Mr. Highcrofft hopefully.

"We got some valuables back there," said Duck. "We got us a saucepot, an' some cups an' saucers."

"But they come from the dump," Mouse reminded him.

"Still them things been valuables ter us," said Duck. "Also got a lef' over piece o' bread. Got them ends o' pencils an' paper wot Robin got fer us." He paused a moment. "But I think 'stead o' goin' back fer them things, an' if Robin don't mind 'bout bits o' pencils, we like 'em ter be gived ter the poor."

"The poor, eh?" said old Mr. Highcrofft, thoughtfully reviewing the boys' clothes, which despire Robin's best sewing efforts, were still little better than rags, not to mention their shoes with flapping soles, holes cut out for toes, and held together with pieces of string.

"Yer church gives ter the poor, don't it?" asked Mouse. "They got this box upstairs wot's full o' money fer the poor. We know 'cause we shooked it an' foun' out."

"Did anything fall out when you ... er ... *shooked* the box?" asked old Mr. Highcrofft with great interest.

"It did," said Spider. "A whole ten cents! But we put it right back in the hole where it come out."

"Why didn't you keep it?" asked the old man.

"Keepin' it would o' been stealin' from the poor," said Piggy. "Even 'fore we stopped stealin' on 'count o' them promises we maked ter the Landlord, we ain't never stealed from the poor. Stealin' from the poor ain't right."

"You're quite right, Piggy, it isn't. I'm sure I don't know why I even suggested you might do such a thing," said old Mr. Highcrofft, turning to his grandson. "You know, Jonathan, I must say I like these boys' style. We might just make it."

"Oh, I think you will, Grandfather," replied his grandson. "But I think it's now really very late, and you'd better all pack yourself into the carriage and head for home."

"Yes, and figure where to put everyone when we get there," said old Mr. Highcrofft.

"You don't need ter worry none 'bout puttin' us anywheres," said Duck. "Jist give us a rag or two ter put under our heads, an' we c'n sleep anyplace you c'n find a piece o' floor ter put us."

"I think we can do a bit better than that, Duck," said old Mr. Highcrofft. "I'm sure Mrs. Delbert . . ." he stopped, throwing a hand to his forehead. "Mrs. Delbert! I don't look forward to seeing the look on her face when I return bringing *this* group with me."

"Why, I've often heard her say she loved boys," said his grandson, with a mischievous grin.

"Oh yes, I'm sure! Thank you so much for your support, Jonathan," said his grandfather. "She will especially love having these four descending on her practically in the middle of the night. Well, come on boys, we'll bear the lioness in her den together."

"Ain't you comin' with us, Robin?" asked Piggy. "I brung yer jacket from the kitchen with mine. It's in the hall."

"Robin will be staying here with us, Piggy," said Jonathan Highcrofft. "I'm sure we'll all be getting together tomorrow, and we'll explain everything to you then. Come on, Robin. I won't ring for Fletcher. We'll see them out ourselves."

So after old Mr. Highcrofft had looked down once more on his great-grandson and kissed the baby's mother lightly on the cheek, he herded the boys from the drawing room into the hall.

As Robin and Jonathan Highcrofft stood waiting for the boys to wiggle into their jackets, they heard Spider saying to Mouse, "Wonder if the place wot we're goin' ter is near as grand as this place."

"Nah, couldn't be," replied Mouse.

"Got eight bedrooms," said Piggy.

"Probable jist countin' big closicks," said Mouse. "Ain't no one in the world got eight bedrooms."

"Oh my," Jonathan Highcrofft said quietly to Robin. "If they think this place is grand, wait until they see Grandfather's house!"

"I expect I'll hear about it tomorrow," said Robin.

"Oh yes indeed, I expect you will!" said Jonathan Highcrofft.

Then as the boys went parading out the door behind old Mr. Highcrofft, this conversation came drifting back to Jonathan Highcrofft and Robin:

SPIDER'S VOICE: "Can't b'lieve wot' happenin' ter us. Must o' been all that holy water we been drinkin'."

DUCK'S VOICE: "Aw shut up, Spider. Ain't you over that? Wot's holy 'bout drinkin' sink water, I arsks you?"

MOUSE'S VOICE: "Well, I jist thinks as how we got ter be dreamin'. Pinch me, Piggy."

(pause)

MOUSE'S VOICE: "Ouch! You don't need ter go pinchin' me so hard, Piggy. It were only dreamin' I arsked to be waked from, not the dead."

PIGGY'S VOICE: "Sorry, Mouse. But now leastways you know you ain't neither."

"Robin, I think we are in for some interesting times, indeed!" said Jonathan Highcrofft.

Chapter XXI

Quite a Story Indeed!

⚜

When Robin returned to the hall with Jonathan Highcrofft, it was also in the company of Adelaide Highcrofft and Danny. They were now ready to go up the winding staircase to the bedrooms, where arrangements were to be made for Danny and Robin.

"Would you like me to send Mrs. Beckett up to you, Adelaide?" Jonathan Highcrofft asked. "I think she can be of great help to you until we find a nurse for Danny."

"Oh, please do send her, Jonathan," said Danny's mother eagerly. "You know, Robin, I confess I don't know the first thing about baby care."

"I can help," Robin said quickly. "Mama taught me how to care for Danny, and I did it when she was so sick before she died. Then after that I took care of him all by myself. If I didn't know how to do it, I might not have dared to run away with him."

All of which reminded Robin of something, and he looked around on the walls for a clock. Unable to find one, he went to where his jacket hung on the coat rack, and pulled out Hawker Doak's watch, which was still in the same pocket. "Danny should be waking up now for his milk," Robin said, after consulting the watch. "We brought his bottles and diapers in the bag that's over there."

"You can't imagine how grateful I am for that," said Danny's mother. "Where would we have found anyplace to get those things tonight? Jonathan, would you please ask Mrs. Beckett to bring along some milk when she comes? Should it be warmed a bit, Robin?"

"Oh, yes!" said Robin, the baby expert. "And you put a drop on your wrist to make certain it's not too hot. Piggy and I always remembered to do that. And put a bit of syrup in with the milk."

"You boys are a wonder!" said Adelaide Highcrofft.

"But Adelaide," said her husband, "do you think you can manage without Robin's help for a few minutes? Mrs. Beckett will be up at once, I'm sure. I have the feeling that with all that's gone on, Robin didn't put away a very big supper and might have room for a little more of that cake, if there's any left. And I'd like to have some with him."

"There *was* a little bit left," said Robin.

"Then you two run along," said Adelaide Highcrofft. "I'll be fine." She came over and kissed her husband lightly on the cheek, then came and did the same to Robin, which caused his heart to skip a beat. Her kiss felt like a butterfly's wings brushing his cheek. And it was done so simply and easily, it was as if she had been doing the same thing all of his life.

"Come along, Robin, let's go summon Mrs. Beckett, and then help ourselves to that good cake," said Jonathan Highcrofft.

"Mr. Highcrofft," said Robin, "may I ask you something?"

"Only if you promise *me* something," he replied. "We can't have you going around calling us Mr. and Mrs. Highcrofft. It just won't do. I know this has all been very sudden, but you'll just have to get used to calling us Mama and Papa, for that's what we're about to be. Do you think you can arrange with yourself to do that?"

"R-right now?" said Robin.

"Why not right now?" asked Jonathan Highcrofft. "It's as good a time as any. And I know it would please Adelaide a great deal."

The delighted Robin took a big swallow. "Then . . . then, Papa, may I ask you something?"

"Fire away," said Jonathan Highcrofft.

"It's about this watch," said Robin, still holding it in his hand. "It belonged to Hawker. He loaned it to me because he sold my watch, the one that belonged to my . . . my first papa. Would you see to it that Hawker's friends Quill and Maggot get it? I expect he would have liked one of them to have it."

"Unfortunately, we have no way of knowing which one," said Jonathan Highcrofft. "And from what I could tell from my brief encounter with those two, I would expect there to be some unpleasantness over it. But I'll do as you ask. You say Hawker sold your papa's watch? Do you know to whom he sold it?"

"He sold it to Mr. Slyke, who has a pawnshop," replied Robin.

Jonathan Highcrofft's eyebrows rose. "Slyke? I know of the man. A very shady character, I understand. Some of my friends' stolen jewelry has turned up at his place of business. I believe he's a dealer in stolen goods. But I'm going to see about getting your watch back for you."

"Mr. Slyke said the watch is only nickel plate," said Robin. "Once I thought I had to sell it myself, because when Hawker sent me to collect rents, one of the people didn't pay enough. Hawker said I had to go back, and I didn't want to. But I was afraid of what he'd do to me, so I took my watch to Mr. Slyke. He said it was only worth twenty-five cents to him. I needed fifty, so I didn't sell it to him. But he only gave Hawker fifteen cents for it, because Hawker didn't care. He only sold it to punish me. But I don't think anyone who buys it from Mr. Slyke should pay much more than that."

"Well, I expect that watch is worth a fair amount more than twenty-five cents. But I don't care what it's worth, because I don't intend to pay Mr. Slyke a single cent for it. And by the time I get through with him, he'll be begging me to take the watch and offering to pay *me* for the privilege. Furthermore, I won't be accepting anything like twenty-five cents. No, he'll be expected to do a great deal better than that! And son," said Jonathan Highcrofft, putting an arm around Robin's shoulders, "that watch is going to be an heirloom you can tell your little brother about some day."

Robin hesitated, and then put his own skinny arm around his new papa's waist, only to feel an answering tightening of the arm around his shoulders. He could hardly wait for the time when he could tell Danny about the watch. For it would have quite a story behind it. Quite a story indeed!

Other Aladdin Mysteries by
BARBARA BROOKS WALLACE

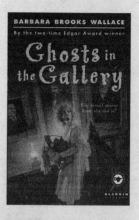

Test your detective skills with these spine-tingling Aladdin Mysteries!

The Star-Spangled Secret
By K. M. Kimball

Secret of the Red Flame
By K. M. Kimball

Scared Stiff
By Willo Davis Roberts

O'Dwyer & Grady
Starring in Acting Innocent
By Eileen Heyes

Ghosts in the Gallery
By Barbara Brooks Wallace

The York Trilogy By Phyllis Reynolds Naylor

Shadows on the Wall

Faces in the Water

Footprints at the Window